THE CAPE MAY STORIES

by ROBERT C.S. DOWNS

WINDSTORM CREATIVE
PORT ORCHARD · WASHINGTON

The Cape May Stories
copyright 2008 by Robert C.S. Downs
published by Windstorm Creative

ISBN 978-1-59092-373-3
9 8 7 6 5 4 3 2
First edition May 2008

Cover by Buster Blue of Blue Artisans Design
Photograph of Cape May Lighthouse stairs by David Lloyd
Photograph of Cape May Lighthouse by Ken Cole

Printed in the United States of America.

For information about film, reprint or other subsidiary rights, please contact:
legal@windstormcreative.com

Windstorm Creative is a multiple-imprint organization involved in publishing books in all genres, including electronic publications; producing games, toys, videos and audio cassettes as well as producing theatre, film and visual arts events. The wind with the flame center is a trademark of Windstorm Creative.

Windstorm Creative
7419 Ebbert Dr SE
Port Orchard WA 98367
www.windstormcreative.com
360-769-7174 ph

Windstorm Creative is a member of the Orchard Creative Group, Ltd.

Library of Congress Cataloging in Publication data available.

For Chris Downs and Bill Rosselli

And for Luca

ACKNOWLEDGEMENTS

The author wishes to thank Cris and Jennifer DiMarco, and the entire staff of Windstorm Creative, for not only accepting this collection of short stories, but also for their careful and dedicated efforts in seeing it through to publication.

THE
CAPE MAY
STORIES

by ROBERT C.S. DOWNS

SHORE LIGHT

At first I think that what awakens my wife and me in this old Cape May Victorian house is the ocean breeze shaking the shades or the distant thunder from the night's storm now far out to sea. But it is not, finally, the weather. It is Gus, our old black Lab sleeping on the floor at the end of our bed who, though in drugged sleep, signals us with several shrill sounds that he is worse this morning than last evening. When he is quiet again I listen for my wife's breathing, which I know instantly is as deep and slow and as fake as mine. We are aware that the other is awake, but, as if in compromise, we remain private. We stay motionless, our elbow, knee and ankle joints as though filled during the night with new, warm fluid, as simple a moment's peace as there is likely to be in this coming day. Between the sweet layers of sleep the soft wind makes small parachutes of the curtains and Helen stirs under the sheet. Then she is still, the heavy summer air an extra blanket on us, and I know that we dread speaking because it will be about Gus and our sons and damned hopeless. Her ankle finds one of mine and lies across it with the weight of a small accident.

Last night, the boys, seven and eight, downstairs watching "Double Thriller Theater," we tried to make love, but it was an amusing failure from the start, two smart people who did not bring their minds to bed. Her head in the middle of my chest, with a tender pat of her hand, she said after a moment's pause, "No good, huh, sheriff?" then raised her head to look at me, her steady eyes the green and blue of special childhood marbles. She lay back and we were silent, our upper arms pressed against each other. Up the huge hollow of the stairwell in this inherited Victorian house poured the screams of still another film victim, and from the sound of his voice, deep and scratched, I imagined him to be about my age, 34, and briefly I wondered how he was done in, and by whom. Then Gus entered the room like a slow fullback, how his shoulder shoved back the door a statement that even though he is nearly blind, riddled with bone problems, and carries his head very low now, he's not quite done yet. He paused, looked at us over the end of the bed, circled, and then went to the floor in organized, heavy sections. "Do you think he'll get through till morning?" Helen asked.

"I hope not," I said.

It would have been easier if Gus had died quietly in the night, but we both know that won't happen now. Today, around five the vet said, she'll come to the house and put Gus to sleep, a smooth needle in the vein over the outside ankle all that it takes.

Through the tall, old windows I see the wet gentleness of the low, racing clouds. Quilt-thick, in an infinite variety of grays, they are in procession eastward, as though they still hear the thunder and now must chase it. All night, in and out of sleep, the storm has been a third person in the room, the 80-year-old panes of glass rattling like boxes of antique combs, the lightning brilliant and, several times, close enough that a transformer on one of the poles a few houses down flashed and spit a huge surge of power. The rain came first, as if from hoses, and then softly, ornamental and friendly, the way a wedding veil might feel if it were made of rain.

Down on the beach now, only a block away, is the sound of a renewed surf, small mountains of dirty, warm slush over and over killing itself on the stiff, packed sand. It is a rotten morning for swimming, debris from the storm intimately arranged throughout the waves, everything from museum-stiff dogfish, to rust-colored seaweed to belly-up horseshoe crabs, from spiked driftwood to dead eels—all in spectacular abundance. By evening the ocean will be calm and clean again, the sedate waves lighted orange and red at their tips from the sunset, something that might last a half second.

Gus stirs now at the end of the bed. Only last year he still had the solid, round strength of the summers when we first started coming here, now almost eight years ago, when he and the boys, no more than toddlers, would endlessly throw themselves in the waves, laughing, nearly suicidal in their abandonment. They and Helen have done better than I have, in their ways, with knowing that Gus was dying. What they have done, that I have not, is sleep with him now and again, when they needed to, the boys in sleeping bags all night on the family room floor, Helen during an occasional afternoon nap on a Saturday, Gus next to her in my place on our bed. My way, in the beginning, was to go from vet to vet, five in as many weeks, first for some confirmation that he would be cured, then verification that he had more time, and finally that he would not suffer much if we let him live out what months might remain.

The vet who's coming was recommended by the Cranemores across the street, who are from Manhattan, and last year had their cat neutered while they were here for the summer. The vet is Korean, and it is already arranged that she will telephone us just before she leaves her office to drive out here. We are to have, according to the segment on a t.v. show we all saw, a home death, our presence to be the first step in the grieving process. Still, as our younger son Louis said after I'd explained, "But Gus is still gonna be dead."

Now there is a small break in the cloud cover and a shot of sunlight through the window smacks a low, curved oblong into the corner of the room. For several seconds it is bright enough to be a new window through which one might see another, lovelier morning. It dims and glows a few times as though breathing, then it is gone, a fresh, dark cloud like a lens cover through the beam. In compensation comes a rush of abundant sea smells, rich enough on the swirling breeze to cause boyhood memories of tall grasses at other beaches, the surprising first taste of salt water, the great weight of a July sun.

Helen stirs again on her side, then struggles with the sheet and blanket to get onto her back, almost makes it, gives up and lies at an angle away from me, only the side of her face available, one eye open and staring as if it is the middle of the night and she has awakened from a mean, unsettling dream. I turn, too, and look up at the ceiling where I can see the long streaks of spackle under the paint, although Helen claims that when I re-did the room it was a perfect job. Shore light, though, is unforgiving, especially in the morning, and in this ancient house there's no repair job that could pass for anywhere near perfect.

Helen turns again, this time the sheet twisting in the fist at her neck, her thick dark hair all over the pillow, and looks at me. "You awake?" she asks.

"No," I answer.

"What am I going to do about my weight?" she says.

"Do you want to get up?"

"Noon," she says. From arthritis that has come unfairly early she already has two fused vertebrae in the iliac area and getting up on mornings when weather has moved through is no fun. Suddenly, noticing the silence, she says, "Is he all right?" A moment follows in which we both listen, our breathing stopped, for some small sound from Gus. He supplies it right away. No doubt plunged into the best part of a running dream, he makes a small grunt, then a muted cry, and we hear his old black broken nails try to grab the bare wood of the floor. "It's right, isn't it?" she asks.

"Don't," I say softly.

"I mean," she goes on, pulling her knees nearly to her waist, "we know he's in pain, right?"

"Dickey said so," I tell her. "Any number of times."

"But how's he know?" she asks.

"A previous life," I say. "Teaching ten-through-twelve English," I go on, "you learn to value outside experts."

"Suppose he's wrong?" she says.

"Then only Gus will know," I answer. I grab a handful of sheet and turn away, curling too. Two feet away I see where a seam in the wall paper has separated right down the middle of a small rose, a crack in the plaster behind it making a tiny bulge so that the base of the flower, for an instant, is palpable and very real.

"I'm sorry," she says, then rests a hand on my shoulder,

its weight feeling like sunlight has found the place. "It's just that we don't have to do it."

"Then when?" I ask.

"Don't be so practical," she says, rolling away. "I hate it when you're like that."

"What'd I say?" I ask.

There is a moment of silence in which the deceptive breeze now sucks the curtains flat against the screens, a little beyond them the tapping of the dry, brittle branches of the young dying maple I planted much too late in the fall three years ago. Then we hear Blake and Billie Cranemore leashing their Yorkie on the front porch, readying themselves, even at this early hour, for a hangover-clearing two miles along the asphalt boardwalk on Beach Avenue. Gus comes along my side of the bed, his head low, his actions the steady performance of a ritual years old now. I touch the side of his head and then pat it twice. Helen, I realize, is watching.

"Billie's ordered a seven-hundred-dollar stationary bike for Blakey's war on cholesterol," Helen says. "A birthday thing." Gus rests his head on the edge of the bed, patiently, his tail in a slow sweep behind him. "I'll do him," Helen says.

I put my hand along her arm, find her hand and hold it loosely for a moment. "I don't mind," I say, and then sit up and swing my legs over.

Downstairs, I go outside with him and stand on the back porch, something that Helen dislikes because I am usually dressed only in boxer shorts and something like what I'm now wearing, a Metuchen Y 5-K benefit race tee shirt, torn under both armpits. He wanders now on his tour out by the huge, unruly lilac bush, always half dead from the winter flooding or spring storms, then along the high hedges at the back of the yard, then over near the Wilberforce's fence, and finally past the free-standing clothes line and to the bottom of the steps. He looks up at me for a moment and then, side to side like an old elephant, he climbs the stairs. Inside the kitchen Helen asks, "Did he do anything?"

"Almost nothing," I answer quietly.

"Suppose he got a diuretic," she says.

"It's just part of it," I tell her. "Look at his eyes."

I turn to see Helen by the counter spooning out the coffee into her pot for decaffeinated, mine next to it already done. Probably she feels the warmth from the hard, early sun that holds her in a gentle, clear light, but certainly she can not be aware of how it has nearly stripped her cotton nightgown so that her legs are perfectly outlined as the grayest and loveliest of shadows.

W e have coffee on our long front porch, one unlike the others along the street because it has a fat fir tree to either side of the steps that gives us some enviable privacy. For a long time it has been what we do in the early mornings, but today, understandably, we are self-conscious and right away at a real loss for words. We sit quietly looking out at the neighborhood, Gus with us at Helen's feet, listening to the patient ocean sounds, waiting for old Mrs. Kronenberger from far down the block to walk by with her nearly blind sister, hand in hand, retired music teachers from Delaware, year-rounders here now.

Looking at Gus, Helen starts to cry in a private, silent way, a couple of tears straight down her cheeks and onto the old lace of her nightgown, and then she stops as if it had never happened, her eyes clear, the track marks drying quickly in the light wind. "What else do they think I'm good for?" she says. Her leap to the previous night's conversation is so sudden that even I am lost for a long moment. "If you're a librarian you're a librarian," she says, now looking straight at Gus, as if he is the one who called her yesterday afternoon about the final decision on reductions come October. "Find another library? Just like that? In these times?" She emphasizes the words strongly enough that a small wave of the coffee flops over the edge of the cup and onto the warped tongue-and-groove of the decking. "If I managed my house," she starts and then abruptly stops and turns once again to look up the street and toward the sliver of ocean where several small waves break like white threads coiling over and over on each other. I do not speak because I know it will do no good. She needs me at this moment to be still. Her other hand rises from the arm of the white wicker chair as though she wishes it to convey a stop message, stays rigid for a few seconds, and then settles back down and rolls over in something like surrender. She swears so softly then that with her head turned the words are lost. "Me without a job," she says. "What's that add up to, huh?" I wait until she turns to look at me, each of us aware that I will again tell her that the high school librarian, Trudy, who is pregnant and may not come back, still wants her part-time. She smiles a little and says, "You're a big help." Then: "That's not a library, it's a lunchroom with bookshelves." She looks away from me to Gus, lets her eyes stay hard and solid on him, then says, "I know, I know." She crosses her legs, ankle over knee, like a man.

It is then that my tongue discovers that during the night I have lost a filling from the inside of my right canine tooth. The hole is ridged and feels enormously deep. I touch the front surface of it and the one next to it with an index finger and know instantly that it does not show and that for now it will do no good to mention it. She glances at me as I make a small, tight sucking sound, then looks away toward the street where Mrs. Kronenberger and her sister, both in identical khaki trousers and sturdy walking shoes, now come along. I turn away to see that in the drops of rain water precariously limp on the very tips of the pine needles there are the fragments of diamonds. The ocean wind now freshens and Gus is the first to notice it, his head up, his snout testing the air, listening. For a long time Helen and I do not speak, then she rises and takes my cup and hers and goes back into the house.

I notice the sagging place over near the edge of the decking that just this year has begun to collect rain water. It means that something underneath, in the complex of supports, perhaps even in the footings or below, has probably broken during the winter or, at least, now has some serious rot. It's evidence of a job that I can not do myself, and I know that I'll delay until the last day here calling Jack Vernon and asking him and his brother to have a look at it after we're gone. They are hunters and, I think, they like Gus more than they like either Helen or me.

Helen comes back out on the porch with our coffee cups filled and sets mine in front of me on the wide railing, it, too, now warped just enough to hold a strand of rain water down its middle the length and depth of a shoelace. The water lies in the sun that slants in brightly behind the tree and no doubt will be gone within an hour. Helen sits down and then pushes her chair back so that it is exactly even with mine. Her feet now can not reach the railing and she crosses them at the ankles, legs straight out. She holds her cup with both hands, thumbs jammed through the handle, the fingers tightly meshed around the front, and looks at Gus, who has not moved. The cup rises and falls on the small, smooth dome of her belly.

"I could do the j.v. cross-country team," I tell her. "The extra comp. would get us close to even."

"It's the smell," she says. "The place, that's all." She turns a little to make brief eye contact. "And Trudy," she says, looking away, "is no librarian." She takes a deep breath and then lets it out slowly through a small narrow space between her lips, the way she exhaled when she smoked. The moment passes, the air suddenly thick with sunshine and now, with a strong wind-shift from inland, the greasy humidity makes itself known. "When did they go to bed?" Helen asks. "I heard them about twelve-thirty."

"Our lives are insignificant to everyone but us," I say.

"A tenth-grader can not plow through Marquez," she tells me, shaking her head. "I don't care what you say."

Our beaches are patrolled in the evening by two sturdy, middle-aged men in white windbreakers who wear blue and white plastic badges and carry fat flashlights that throw long, wide beams. Just after sunset, though, earlier when the mosquitoes swarm if the air is still, they disappear into the bars and sidewalk restaurants down in the middle of the town. At the various entrances to the beach there are signs that give these men purpose. There is a *NO* three feet high on one side, then opposite a list of things in smaller letters: Fishing, Alcohol, Surfing, Fires, Dogs. Benevolently, on the bottom, are the restrictions 9 A.M. To 9 P.M. There is less than an hour now for Gus's morning walk, and as we go down the steps and across the street he knows, because both of us are with him, that this is an unusual day. I wonder if he thinks that this is the day we are going home, or if our cousins from Connecticut are due, or if he thinks that, like last week, he will again be allowed the banquet of scents at the veterinarian's. He walks between us, half his body in front, exactly at our pace.

Our sons, of course, are taking it much better than we. Our talk with them, although we prepared as if for an inaugural address, lasted not more than ten minutes, the only area of contention being the business of Gus's dying on our front porch. Louis set his small, perfect jaw to the side and asked why the porch. Gary, his senior by 15 months, whose heart already belongs to the sciences, impatiently explained about the bladder. Louis looked at him in suitable horror, and then said, "Disgusting."

The beach sand is still wet and heavy from the rain, evidence of how furious it was in the perfectly shaped shallow bullet holes everywhere drying from the center out. As we walk a crust forms on the soles of my old running shoes, and in spite of Helen's sandals dark sand lies in small, comfortable pockets between her toes. We watch Gus as though we expect it is possible that he will give us a symbolic, important sign, a signal across the species that confirms some unspoken, enduring principle. Of course, Gus does no such thing. He noses an empty bag of corn chips between two Bud cans, then a wad of brown seaweed, and finally, and stupidly, he laps some seawater. Unmistakably, though, there is still a fine jiggle to his muscles, especially in the hind quarters, and now and then as we go along he raises his head in answer to something we can not know. For a while we see some other morning regulars with their dogs, nod or lift a hand to say hello, and then surprisingly the whole place is empty in a stark, wide way, the slant of the beach to the water as though we are privileged now to feel the curve of the earth. Gus moves very slowly, running out of steam already, Helen says, then looks at me, and we stop and sit on some rounded rocks.

"It *was* my mother on the phone last night," Helen says. When I only nod she goes on with, "I didn't want to worry you. I'm sorry." Her mother's calls have become increasingly less lucid in the last two years, and sometimes when trying Helen's sister's number she mistakenly dials ours. Helen wants to confront her on the matter, but I have disagreed, and from time to time it has caused some small sparks between us. "She's in her sixties," I usually say, "and can balance her checkbook faster than both of us. Leave her alone." Now Helen lets it go with, "I just wanted you to know."

"Maybe you should ask Maureen if she does it with her," I say.

"Think she'd own up?" Helen asks, smiling. She slides a foot from her sandal and then sticks the big toe into Gus's neck hair far enough that it disappears. He takes no notice.

"Not Maureen," I say.

"What gets me," Helen says, her eyes straight out to the horizon, hands jammed into her jeans pockets up to the thumbs, "is the goddamn routine." She half turns her head toward me but her eyes stay exactly where they were. I nod just enough to know that she sees my agreement. When she is upset, usually when she does not have control of something important, she takes a swipe at the commonplace, as though some particular problem, like Gus now, has been intentionally imposed on her alone. It does not last long.

"We'll be there with him," I say, then pause, then make the mistake of adding, "The vet even asked if we'd want to assist."

She puts her full attention on me now. "Could you?" she asks.

"I once shot a pigeon with a pellet gun," I say. "Took two

hits, though."

"Such pride," she answers, looking away.

"Not having him around is going to be murder," I tell her.

"I know," she says.

It is then that Louis comes racing down the beach toward us, hands waving, something clearly wrong. In the few seconds he takes to sprint across the sand Helen and I glance at each other, our thoughts instantly on what in the name of God has happened to Gary. The answer comes quickly from Louis that he has fallen on the stairs and has cut his head. "He's bleeding," Louis says, a hand up in the direction of the house.

"Is he all right?" I ask, and Louis looks at me like he's just discovered that I am, in fact, a teacher.

"What daddy means," Helen says with ultimate calm, "is whether Gary is awake. Conscious."

"Sure," Louis says.

"Where's the cut?" Helen asks. Louis leans over, as if he has one, too, and puts his hand squarely on the top of his head. "Let's go," Helen says, and together they start to run across the sand. It is understood that I will follow along with Gus, who now stands, front section first, his rear rising awkwardly as though his left hip and leg are dead asleep and he can not feel them.

Walking along the sandy sidewalk toward the house I see that during the storm three more cedar shingles from the siding have popped off and now lie on the lawn next to the foundation. The small squares from the uncovered wood gleam in the sun like finger tips of new flesh. Nearing the house it seems that Gus hears the crying before I do, and in what way he can he quickens his walk. When I finally hear it I hurry on ahead and up the stairs into the front hall. Gary has cut his head, all right, and in precisely the place Louis described. It looks and, with Gary's wailing, sounds much worse than it is. Helen has a stack of small kitchen towels and a bowl of pink water on the floor next to the heating grate, and is kneeling in front of Gary, who sits cross-legged and bent over at forty-five degrees, offering her his head. Louis has his arms folded so tightly that he looks cold, his face set in a determined way. When I ask him softly what happened he releases one arm and points to the stairs where the heavy, wide banister has lost two of its supports and where the bottom post now leans slightly to the side. In our early years here they played on it, sliding five and six feet down it, the smallness of their bodies and the sturdiness of the oak making it safe. I see, too, where for six inches or so along the old, wide baseboard there is blood from where his head struck. Against the white of the paint it is curiously and awkwardly bright.

"Why now?" I ask Gary, his head draped and invisible. He looks like a boxer after a bad loss.

"He did it, too," Gary says.

I look at Louis who turns and holds me in a stare that startles me with its anger. "I did," he says coolly. "That's true."

"But why?" I ask. His delicate, angular face stays adult and passive, and there is not the slightest sign that he is contrite. I stare at Louis for a long moment, and then Gary says from under the towel, "He went first." Almost simultaneously, Helen quietly says, a quick glance at me, "It's just Gus." I turn to look at the front door where he now stands staring in from the other side of the screen. In the rising morning light he seems only another shadow, one with ash-colored eyes.

When Helen finishes with Gary she guarantees both boys some Diet Pepsi and a plate of Chips-Ahoy if they'll wait for her with Gus on the porch. They obey like eager soldiers, and when they are outside she looks up at me and smiles a little, then shakes her head at the mess that's been made. "Scalp wounds," she says, "sure do bleed a lot." I tell her that if she'll get the snacks I'll clean up. "Sold," she says and goes by me to the back of the house.

Gary's blood on the baseboard is not yet dried, but it has congealed on the paint and there is some of it wedged into the spaces between the pieces of molding. Getting all of it up proves a more difficult task than I thought, and I have to use my thumb nail to take away the dried edges completely. When I finish and go back to the kitchen, Helen already out on the front porch, I put the soaked paper towels in the trash under the sink and turn on the water to wash my hands. Then I stop and look down at the blood and I think this is my blood, too, and Helen's, and I stand very still right there and give myself the pleasure of making two solid fists. Then I make a picture in my mind of the coming night, the boys asleep early, Helen and me on top of the sheets in a white moonlight. We have made love, have kissed each other for a long time, something unusual for us lately, and I am just able to see the way our bodies shine.

GRIEF AND FIRE

So expected on this Saturday morning is the death of Helen's dearest, life-long friend that she has fled the house early so she will not have to take the phone call when it finally comes. Last night, before we left Metuchen to drive down here, Tildy's husband called from Boston to say she was awake and very alert. "Full of fight," I heard as Helen broke and handed me the phone to listen to more words, resigned and compassionate, truly meant to help. All night, through a thin spring rain, we hardly slept, our sons, eight and ten, anxious and testing past midnight until they gave out and, to calm themselves, finally went to bed in one twin, limbs loose and, in sleep, sure to touch each other in a blessed, ignorant way.

From the porch, naive and useless, I watch Helen go. She walks to the corner, sandals unbuckled and flopping, arms folded tightly, underdressed in shorts and sweatshirt on this cool, gray day. As she turns on Philadelphia and goes up toward the low, flat motels along Beach Avenue, two strangers, a woman and a boy, approach her coming this way. When they stop and speak to her and she keeps going I know already she is crying hard and doesn't give a damn who sees it. The woman is small, round, and kind-looking, about my age, beside her what I assume is her son, perhaps 12, or even 13. He is no taller than she, but clearly inside his square build there is a coming maturity. His tan jacket open, he has his hands deep in the pockets of his gray khakis. A red necktie, its end four inches below his belt, looks like an exclamation point. She's in a blouse and white sweater with long sleeves, a navy blue skirt with sturdy black walking shoes, and carries a large over-the-shoulder bag, like a meter maid's. They hesitate at the corner and then start my way, the woman with a wide, warm smile, the boy to her outside, cautious, his hands still stuffed. I assume they are pleasant missionaries of one kind or another, that I will thank them politely for stopping, which they'll understand and then be on their way. The woman moves a little ahead as they turn from the sidewalk to come to our front steps. Now I see that while their clothes are remarkably clean, and the boy's pants have a sharp crease, the age of what they wear is in his frayed collar and the outline of her thighs through the shiny fabric of her skirt.

She removes a clipboard from her bag and astonishes me by reading our names in a formal, distant way: "Henderson, Jack and Helen?" When I nod slowly, she says, "May I ask you a few questions?"

"About?" I answer, wary.

The boy smiles, his teeth perfect, brown eyes large and clear. "I'm Frederick," he says, and the woman looks at him with pride.

"Marketing information," she answers, turning the

clipboard to show a full-page questionnaire. When I tell her quickly I'm not interested in buying anything, and then add we're here only for today and tomorrow, she says, "We get eight dollars a client."

I look over their heads toward Philadelphia Avenue, where Helen has gone, and of course there is no sign of her. "Okay," I say and move away to the two aluminum beach chairs to the left. Frederick takes the steps two at a time, as though this were his porch, hoists himself onto the railing and hooks his feet through the spindles, trapeze-style. She gives me a white card with shiny, raised type that says her name, Margaret Stone, underneath it Collins and Associates, Marketing Consultants, Inc. She says they represent the Acme in the center of town and then makes a small recitation of how the market is considering expansion and the company needs the information in order to best advise the executives in Trenton. "Might double," she says, smiling, relieved.

As she takes a pen from under the metal clip at the top of her board I see her hands are unlike the rest of her, young, backs like white stones in a stream, cuticles and nails as though just from the manicurist. Then as she writes down the time and date I ask her how she got my name and she says the company uses the city tax rolls. She points with the pen at the houses to either side of us, consults a second sheet, then says the names of those two neighbors.

All business, she begins the questions, which I answer in a voice flat and remote: 36; high-school English teacher; about $33,000; 36; part-time librarian; about $8,500; two boys, their ages. Then about the house: 1914; owned eight years; no mortgage; inherited; summer rentals. "We're here this weekend to clean," I offer.

I turn to see Frederick staring at me. "Can I have a glass

of water?" he asks. I smile, point to the door, and tell him to go straight down the hall to the kitchen on the right. When he goes inside Mrs. Stone's questions become specific about our grocery-buying habits, and, although I shop, too, I am uneasy about giving her wrong information and qualify much of what I say. Although it is only a little past nine, I think how tired she looks, how laboriously she prints the answers and circles the tiny numbers, the tip of her tongue pressed hard into the corner of her mouth.

When the phone rings it startles both of us, but before I can get to the screen door I hear Frederick answer it. He hands me the phone and says, "Aunt Maureen." I think he's on his way out to the porch but he surprises me by going straight into the front room to my left and over to the television, which he turns on. "Any news?" Maureen asks, and I tell her no, nothing this morning, but that Grant called last night and there's nothing left except the waiting. "It's going to wreck her," Maureen says, her voice with the helplessness of a sister far away. Frederick stands mostly on one leg, head cocked to the side, staring at a cartoon while I reassure Maureen that as soon as we hear we'll call. Then as I hang up Frederick gives the television a very emphatic finger, holding it out and up as though the characters on the screen might actually be able to see it. "You're too old for those shows," I say.

"Tell me about it," he answers, and as he shifts his weight to the other foot, the phone rings again. It's Helen, and in her voice there is years of distance. "Anything?" she asks, expecting the worst because she's tried to call while I've been talking with Maureen. I tell her no, and explain, and she is quiet for a time. She says she's down at Convention Hall on the boardwalk and intends to keep going, probably all the way out to the beach at the Point, a five-mile walk. It is an empty, wide, wind-blown place with swaying tall grass that, so she has said, has a thousand places to lie down. She asks if that's all right and I say of course it is. When I tell her the boys are still asleep she reminds me there's eggs with bacon for them. She sounds lost and I imagine she turned from the phone to look out over the ocean at an endless gray sky, light purple and shot through with white, as though it is still midwinter. "It's where I want to be," she says. The remoteness in her voice increases, the sound as if from the center of a fleeing galaxy, and I remember the way her face looked, how the tiny muscles went slack as though severed when I had to tell her nine years ago her father, Mel, died. Holding her, I said I knew how she felt, as thoughtless a statement as could be made, and she was swift to answer, her fingers digging into my arms, "You *couldn't.*"

"I'll find you," I tell her, but so quick is she to hang up I know she doesn't hear what I've said, or care. In her way, she has told me she wants me to bring the final news of Tildy to her later, out where there isn't anyone and she can finally let it all go. Briefly, but with no success, I try to imagine what even a small part of the great weight she carries must feel like.

Mrs. Stone calls out Frederick's name, which is easy to hear through the open front door, and he answers that he's going to watch t.v. until she's finished. Then I ask him how many people his mother interviewed this morning. "Mrs. Stone's my foster mom," he says.

"And your real family?" I ask.

He says his mother and stepfather were killed in a car crash last winter, then looks back at the t.v. and adds he has a brother who was adopted and now has to live in Avalon. Then his eyes come back to mine and he smiles. "I go everywhere with her," he says proudly.

When I go back outside I tell Mrs. Stone right away what a shame it was to learn about Frederick's parents. "He's a fine boy," she says. "Caring." Her eyes drift along the porch, then across the yard to the house next door. She takes the top sheet from the clipboard and buries it on the bottom of the pile, then readies another page of questions. "Did he also tell you I'm trying to find a home for him?" she asks. Slowly, I shake my head, then shift in the chair and cross my legs. "You're certainly the right age," she says.

"No, no," I answer, shaking my head, forcing a small smile.

"Why not?" she asks.

Defensively, I start to tell her about what the morning has been like, and last night, too, and how, actually, I'm just waiting to hear my wife's friend has died. She is clearly affected and keeps her soft, steady eyes on me. I look away and toward the sky where the clouds seem to have stopped. In my mind Helen sits on the steep part of the beach at the Point, arms around her knees, cheek down on them, or lies among the high grass, hands tight behind her head, staring at the same sky.

When I ask Mrs. Stone if she knew Frederick before the accident, or was a relative, she says no, fostering is something she started doing after her husband died. "Frederick's number twenty-two," she says. "All placed."

Although I can not see him, and have no basis for knowing it is so, I feel Frederick watching me through the window. I shift in my chair and cross my legs the other way. I want the telephone to ring, the boys to awaken, breakfast to be required of me, the house cleaning for the early rentals to begin the way we do it every year.

"You're a nice man," Mrs. Stone says. "Your wife, too, I imagine." I stare at her, my breathing a little fast now but

under control. "You'd do very well with Frederick," she
says.

"We can't," I tell her.

"Won't," she says.

"Does that matter?" I ask.

"Not to me," she says.

Then, methodically, she checks over the pages of the
questions she's asked, the tip of her pen darting here and
there to make certain her information is complete. When
she calls to Frederick to come out, that they're leaving, he
opens the screen door so quickly that I know he's been
listening behind it. He lets the door close on its own and
stands, one hand holding the other in front of the bottom of
his tie. I study him for a long moment in an embarrassing,
open appraisal. Just when it occurs to me he's feeling
rejected, that his own self-esteem must be at a terrible low
point, he says, "What's wrong with you, mister?" I wait for
Mrs. Stone to reprimand him, but she only looks at me
sternly, as if he has asked the question for her, too. Then the
moment is shattered by the telephone, and I excuse myself
as though we still had more to say, then realize we do not,
and raise my hand to say goodbye.

Inside, just before I answer the phone, I see their heads
disappear going down our steep steps. I take a breath and
pick up the receiver. As I expected, it's Grant. He
acknowledges me, then asks for Helen. It runs through my
mind that this is proper to do, and when I tell him she isn't
here he will go ahead and give me the details. Then I hear
him quietly say, away from the phone, "She's gone out,"
then nothing, then finally, and amazingly, with the identical
distance of how Helen sounded, Tildy speaks. Her voice is
weak, but the enunciation is perfect, the words formed as
though she spent a long time preparing them. She is also

very short of breath. "Jack, tell her I love her," she says slowly.

"I will," I answer as if it were a wedding vow.

"Have her call when she gets home," she says.

"Of course," I tell her, but the words go to Grant, who has taken the phone, and who simply, sadly, says my name. "How's she doing?" I ask, knowing how empty I sound.

"Good, real good," he answers the same way.

"I'll tell Helen," I say.

"Do that," he says, "and thanks." Then he hangs up.

I open the door and go out on the porch. Mrs. Stone is looking up at me from the sidewalk, Frederick across the street waiting for her, leaning against a tree. "Is Helen's friend dead?" she asks. The use of her name is almost too intimate to bear and I look at Mrs. Stone for a long moment, as if just realizing I've known her in some different form for a lifetime. When I shake my head she smiles, raises her right hand from which her first two fingers loosely extend, as if she means an intentional blessing, and then turns to cross the street to go to Frederick. Head down, she does not see him give me the finger, his face tight with rage, anything childlike about him instantly gone. Confused, I watch for a while as they try several other houses on the block, all still closed for the winter, and then turn the corner and go back down Madison toward Beach Avenue.

In the house I switch off the television, and, as I turn to go down the hall toward the kitchen, I see both our sons standing at the bottom of the stairs in their camouflage pajamas. Their faces are empty of color, eyes wide with questions, as if they think I am perfect and can make their whole world right with a few words. Gary, tough and direct, says, "Did Aunt Tildy die?"

"No," I answer.

"She's gonna be all right," Louis tells him.

"Warlock," Gary answers.

"She *is*," Louis says, his eyes up at me, as if he believes I alone can make it so.

Simultaneously, they realize that Helen is not home, and they are clearly uneasy about it. When Gary asks, as if it is a challenge, where she is, I tell them she's gone to the Point, then add because it's where she can feel close to Tildy. "Huh?" Gary says.

"When's she coming back?" Louis asks, his eyes suddenly loaded with tears. I answer that later in the afternoon we'll get some fried chicken from the Filling Station in town, and a couple of orders of fries, too, and go out to meet her for a picnic on the beach. This confuses them more because it's what we have done only on the last Sunday afternoon at the end of September when we've come down to close the house. They solve the problem by turning on the television.

As I make eggs and bacon, the noise from their precious cartoons is everywhere downstairs. I start to cry twice but each time hold back, my eyes like Louis's were, my breath gone, swallowed. They eat on the floor in front of the television, legs tightly crossed, the four English muffins with peanut butter gone in a flash. For the next couple of hours, to be near them, I wash the windows in the room, then move across the hall to the other front room, identical in size and number of windows. I do some touch-up woodwork painting in both rooms, and when I think I might be able to run the vacuum and still hear the telephone, it rings. My first thought is that it is Helen and she is at the phone booth next to the hot dog stand at the Point and wants to be picked up now.

It is Grant, and it is over. He tells me in a terrible flat voice, as though somehow experienced in these matters, that it was peaceful, that, really, she was there one moment, gone the next. Then he says where and when the service is going to be, the plans, it seems, made days, if not weeks, ago. He says it would mean a lot if we could come up for it, and I tell him of course we'll be there. When I ask if he's all right he grunts in a kind, lost way and says, "Ask God, pal."

When I hang up it takes a moment to realize the boys have heard everything. They turn to look at me, Louis first, then Gary, their eyes dumping tears down their motionless, pale faces. They look abandoned, as though it is Helen who has died, and when Gary asks me what it's like to die, Louis glancing at him as though he wishes to speak those words, too, I stare at them both for a long time. As honestly as I can, I say, "I don't know," and on their faces is a disappointment the likes of which I have never seen. When Gary says his teacher told them it's when your body doesn't work anymore I say, eager to agree, "That's right, it's like that."

But Louis is not so quickly satisfied. Pensive and introspective, he looks up at me for a long moment, then says, "What's it like to have someone die?" His eyes go instantly to Gary, who turns to him slowly, awkwardly, in response to the question. There is a moment in which each attempts to process such an impossible consideration, then they abandon it and look squarely at me.

"I don't know," I answer softly, and they turn back to the television while I stand helplessly trying to imagine what Helen would say to them now.

On the way to the Point in the car with the boys I see Mrs. Stone and Frederick on the corner of Washington and Madison, indecisive, she pointing down toward town, he the other way. Just as I look to my left to see when the bank will hold Saturday hours for the summer, Frederick bolts into the street between two cars, right into the path of a turning pickup truck. It's moving so slowly it seems nothing at all serious can possibly happen. There is even time for me to think that the driver, when he finally brakes, ought to lean out his window and give the kid hell. Then the left front fender hits Frederick in the side and he corkscrews to the pavement, his legs wound helplessly around each other. The right front tire rides over his midsection as though it has done nothing more than take a speed bump in a school parking lot, and then the truck stops so abruptly its front bumper nearly hits the ground.

Mrs. Stone, and everyone else, is frozen in the moment. Then she walks dumbly into the street toward him, falls on her knees in the crosswalk, and sadly, with nothing left, tries to crawl to him. One arm reaches out, the hand bent up to a right angle, fingers twisted as if it is she who has been hit by the truck. She moves forward so slowly it appears she will never reach him, that she is suspended in some special place and time which has no exit.

As the boys and I get out of the car the driver of the pickup opens his door and jumps down to the street where he stares at Frederick, now lying face down, his lower legs partly under the truck. Two cars make quick turns and speed off, one in front of us, the other from behind the truck, and no one seems to care at all. The boys stand next to me, their eyes brown dull jewels. Then Frederick raises his head and brings his arms in front to support his upper body, and looks over at Mrs. Stone still at least ten feet from him. Using his elbows, he pulls himself from under the truck, rises into an urgent, awkward crouch, his fingers still on the asphalt, and goes to her as fast as he can.

Frederick does not appear to be hurt. The truck tire, it's plain to see on his jacket, went right between his ribs and hips, and the ease and quickness with which he moves to Mrs. Stone says he has no reason to have concern for himself. When he gets to her she straightens so she is on her knees to receive him, arms weakly out, her face as though she has just seen hell. They embrace for a long moment, both on their knees, Mrs. Stone sobbing helplessly. Then she eases back from Frederick, one hand holding his shoulder, the other flat against her forehead, as if she is forced in her mind to see it all happen again and again.

"I'm sorry," Frederick says. "I'm sorry I did that to you." He looks down at her hand on his shoulder, hesitates, then turns his head to kiss it.

The pickup driver persuades Mrs. Stone to let him take them to the emergency room, and as they drive away Gary folds his arms across his chest, the way mine are, and steps out into the street to watch the truck go. Louis looks at him with wonder. When I tell them the boy and the woman came by the house this morning, and that the boy watched television while they slept, there is a moment of disbelief, then Gary says to Louis, "I told you."

"Why?" Louis asks me, ignoring Gary. I tell him the two reasons Mrs. Stone was there, but I see right away he does not understand *demographic*, nor does Frederick's situation mean anything, either. "Why'd she pick you?" Louis asks.

"I was just on the porch," I answer. "Available."

As we drive down Lafayette Street, which goes through town and leads straight out to the Point, I realize the Filling Station doesn't open until late afternoon this early in May. When Gary asks if we can go over the bridge to the Burger King in North Cape May I tell him no, it's the other way. Their response is to sing a brief snatch of the Burger King commercial and then poke each other and giggle. They seem so free.

The small parking area at the Point between the shell shop and the hot dog stand is empty, the old five-foot lengths of railroad ties that mark the parking spaces still at odd angles from winter flooding. The thin coating of sand over the pocked asphalt is glass-smooth and pristine, sea debris everywhere, gulls as still as lawn statues. Even the boys sense how new the place feels. As we go down onto the beach, Louis's hand in mine, Gary running ahead and spinning in anxious circles, Tildy's dying hits me like nothing ever before. First comes a weight I have never known, or even imagined, then the whitewater of adrenaline and a true terror, as if I'm allowed to know only for an instant that grief and fire are the same thing.

A few moments later I see Helen so far down the beach that at first I can't tell which way she's walking. The boys see her, too, and, yearning to be with her, run wildly ahead. When they get to her she kneels and hugs both at the same time so that they lean over backwards in relief and pleasure, their arms dangling toward the sand. As I approach, the boys take each other's hand, something I have not seen for years, and hurry off to play foot tag with the small, dying waves. From about five feet in front of me Helen says, arms slightly out to the side, "What am I going to do without her?" My answer is to shake my head very slowly, mute and empty. There is a flash of rage that passes through her, her fists small rocks, eyes wide and lunatic-like for an instant, mouth open in a wordless statement of awe at how the anger makes her feel. Then she is limp, her chin nearly on her chest, her hair a crude veil, and finally she is crying at her core in a tearless, primitive way.

I see then that not only are her sandals gone, her feet

bare and coated with sand, but there are small cuts on the insteps and arches of both, the kinds of scratches I know the jetty rocks can make, or that could have come from some of the thorny shrubbery high up along the beach. As she brings her crying under control she appears even more vulnerable, as if Tildy's death claimed some small, dear part of her, too. When she looks up at me, her eyes are hugely dark and strangely beautiful, as if during the day she has removed herself to a silent, safe place near the edge of sanity. She turns to watch the boys splash in the cold tidal puddles, and, for a long few moments, she seems desperate to set this moment permanently in her mind, our tiny world photograph-stiff and hers forever.

"Where're your sandals?" I ask.

Still looking at the boys, she tells me the left one fell into the water while she was out on the rocks, and that it only seemed natural to chuck in the other one, too. "You can't really help me," she says.

"I can take care of your feet," I tell her.

It's then she seems to notice them for the first time. She lifts a foot sideways, by her other knee, and looks at it, her hand holding the toes, and along the arch there is a small gash that has been closed over by the cold. There is a similar wound on the other foot in nearly the same place, as though she stood for a long stubborn time on the edge of something much sharper than the rocks. I take her hand to walk down the slope to the water's edge and she holds mine very tightly as though, in these last hours, she has learned to fear the ocean. In the water her feet go ivory-white and amazingly cold, and here and there blotches of blue, like disease, appear on the arches, then the tops.

"Can you feel anything?" I ask, my hands around both ankles.

"No," she answers.

I look up to see her arms are folded and she stares straight out across the water toward Lewes, miles and miles away. I tell her to sit down a little way up where the sand is dry, and when she does I kneel in front of her, open my jacket and shirt, put both feet on my chest, and hold her legs behind the knees, her elbows small fulcrums in the sand. She closes her eyes. The boys, who think we are playing a game, hurry over and put themselves to either side of me, then Gary hangs for a moment around my neck and Louis leans his back against mine. Gary speaks to her first. "We saw an accident by the bank," he says.

"A boy got runned over by a car," Louis adds quickly.

Helen's eyes snap open and she stares at him in a way that makes him anxious and a little frightened.

"Walked away from it," I say, and shake my head. "Amazing."

Against my skin, Helen's feet press in painfully now, as though they are stones from the sea. After several more long moments, though, the cold draining into my chest, her feet begin to warm. She looks straight at me, her grief suddenly, temporarily gone, as if it has tired of such a complete and victorious possession.

"What did Grant say?" she asks.

I tell her about the service next Tuesday, what's planned, say that maybe we ought to call the sitter from here before we go home tomorrow to set things up for overnight. She glances away to where the boys dig with their hands in the sand, oblivious of us. "I loved her so," she says, once more starting to show the grief. Then, as if she simply wills it to be, she controls the great wave of feeling inside her.

"I talked to her," I say. "Grant put her on for a moment." She asks what Tildy said, and when I hesitate briefly she says, "The exact words. I want to have them."

"She said, 'Tell her that I love her,'" I say, and then watch her eyes close briefly. I smile a little as I hesitate, then finish with, "And that you're to call when you get home."

"Then she couldn't have known it was so close," she says, her eyes widening in mild surprise.

"Does that matter?" I ask.

"Yes. It means she thought she had more time," she says, "maybe even some days or a week." She pauses, then adds, "It means she didn't have to look it smack in the face."

I lift her foot to glance at the cut on the underside of the arch, red but already in the first stage of healing, and just before I softly press my lips to it I understand why Frederick, rising from under the wheel of that truck, wished only to kiss the hand of Mrs. Stone. Then, finally, I can say to her, "Like you have."

STOP SIGNS

Because our long-standing June rental, a Penn professor and his wife, cancelled because of his bypass surgery, Helen and I are here trying to paint all 13 rooms in the two weeks our sons, 11 and 13, are at camp up in Port Jervis. An unexpected dividend of being here is that tonight we'll get to see what the Cranemores across the street call the famous all-night party given annually by 75-year-old Colonel and Cleo Wilberforce next door. It's always on June 21, so the colonel himself told us this morning when he came over to say that if things got too loud just to give him a call. "On the longest day of the year," he said. Then, curiously, he winked and added, "Old sport," then turned and left. So, for the last half hour, bone-tired, we've been here on the porch waiting, hoping the cool evening wind off the ocean will keep the mosquitoes down.

As though cued, two spotlights high on the front of the

house come on as the first car approaches—an old yellow MG, probably around '52, top down, a couple as old as the Wiberforces in it, heads back, laughing. I look up from the curb to see the colonel come out onto the porch—identical to ours, both houses having been built by the same man— and walk down the steps to the street. In the shimmering white light from the spots I have no trouble seeing that he's dressed in a navy-blue blazer, white ducks, white shirt, and is wearing, with it proudly flared an inch or two, the necktie of the local yacht club. As he greets the first couple, and then stands chatting with them, others arrive, each in a distinctive car, most, like the MG, antiques, and the couples who emerge from them are in no significant way different either in age or dress from the first one. Probably within not more than twenty minutes thirty to forty cars line New York Avenue. So prompt are they that it is as though someone's large dinner party has just let out.

It's as the string quartet appears from inside the house— three middle-aged women in black, and a young bald man— that our phone rings in the front hall. While Helen gets it, I watch a gentle flow of traffic start inside the house. Champagne, wine, liquor and canapes are served by waiters in white gloves who circulate with small silver trays, and out on the porch, dimly lighted from the music stands, there are the on-off red dots of a few cigars and cigarettes. Now and again over the music comes the sound of older laughter.

I don't know Helen's back until I feel her hand on my shoulder, and when I turn to look up her eyes are wide with tears, on her face an expression close to what she looked like when I had to tell her Mel died. "God," I say so softly that with the music she probably doesn't hear me, "what is it?" She sits on the arm of the rocker and takes my hand, then says it was the camp director and Gary and Louis are—and

here she pauses and then says as if she were reading it—
along with eight others, missing on a hike. She presses her
thumbs into the back of my hand, swallows hard, the
shadows along her throat rolling, then says that the director
told her everything was under control, a search of the area
has been on for some hours now. "Some hours?" I say. "He
said, '*Some* hours'?" She nods as her eyes settle on the wall
behind me, seeing absolutely nothing. "Let's go," I say, then
come forward in the chair and almost stand before I realize
the uselessness of my words.

As she says the director told her he'd call back with an
update in a couple of hours her face starts to come apart
and quickly she covers it with her hands. I swear a couple of
times, then smack the heels of my hands on the ends of the
rocker arms. When Helen takes her hands away her face
looks as though she's just felt an enormous pain she can't
even begin to control. Then, with no conviction at all, I try
to reassure her the boys will be all right. I remind her how
much we liked the place and the people, that the director
said last year that they've never even had a broken arm in
ten years. Finally, stupidly, I say we can't panic, above all we
can't do that. "Dear God," is all she says.

About eleven, the only thing different is that I've found
the 30-foot extension cord some renter put on the
phone last year, hooked it up, and brought the phone out
on the porch where it now sits on the decking between us.
When it rings Helen has it in her hand and up to her ear in
less than a second, but after she says hello she goes silent for
a long time. Watching her, I realize I'm having trouble
breathing, that my chest has gone still, my heart pounding.
Then Helen, saying only, "We'll be here," puts the phone

back down and says slowly, "Nothing. Not a thing." From nowhere I start my reassurance again, but Helen stops me by putting a hand on my arm and gesturing with her head to the back porch of the Wilberforce's house where a couple are kissing, arms around each other as far as they can go. After a few seconds it's clear that this is a kiss that means business, and when the man breaks it off and moves his lips down to the woman's neck I realize I've never seen two people, certainly in their seventies, doing anything like this. It is a strange sight at first, but then how they kiss and caress and look each other straight in the eyes gives them no age at all. They could be any couple on Earth.

"They're five hours from here," Helen says. "We're never doing that again."

She's quiet as we watch the couple from the back porch come down onto the lawn and walk, hand in hand, to their Jaguar convertible. He opens the door for her, waits as she gets in, then shoves it closed with both hands. "They're not going back next year," she finally says. I add not on your life. "There's the beach," she says, "the fishing." I tell her I'll take them myself, just like I used to. She picks up the phone and sets it in her lap, both hands holding it. Then, once more, she starts to cry, but this time there is no hysteria; rather, the tears flow freely, as if they serve no other purpose than to cleanse.

Then quietly, Helen first, we exchange long-forgotten, minor stories about their childhoods—how Gary got sick in Wendy's one evening, the way Louis caught a fly ball with his head in Little League tryouts, the time Gary said he lost his fourth-grade report card because he'd made a C in math, the afternoon Louis got so mad at me that he ran away to live in the garage. Helen turns slightly toward me and smiles, the lights from the party pale and angular on her face. "They'll be all right. I know they will," she says. I don't answer but, rather, force a smile and nod just once. She holds my eyes with hers and then, from nowhere, says, "Ever run a stop sign?" I think this is her effort at a light moment and I answer that I've done my share of roll-throughs. She says I mean really run it. I shake my head and tell her not on purpose, no. She tells me that the year before we met she did it once, just blasted right through the thing at about 40-45. I wait a moment, then ask why. She says that to this day she doesn't know, but that maybe it had something to do with giving up control. At least that's what she felt in the moment. She says there was a kind of surrender in it she'd never known before. I ask her if she thought of what she could have done to someone else and she nods, then says only afterwards.

She moves the phone a little in her lap, then asks me if I ever wanted to be something other than an English teacher—like, she says, did I ever think of the Ph.D. and did getting married when we did stop me. I say no, I'm doing what I want to be doing, then ask where'd that come from? She says she's not sure, it's just that she's thought that sometimes she was holding me back. I tell her I'm not going to go and get a Ph.D. at my age, especially when I don't want one. You're the one who never finished the MLS, I say. She surprises me by saying that she thinks she might go back in the fall and take one of the last three courses. "It'd be at night," she says.

"Good," I say, "good." Then I ask her why now and she says she knows that if it's not soon she'll never do it. "And you'd get a great raise from the library," I tell her.

"Oh, for sure," she says.

At a little after two the colonel's party still shows no signs of winding down. I tell Helen if I were their age, and drinking like that, I'd have fallen over three hours ago. It is a wonder, she says. Right then a white van slides into the driveway between our houses, *Gloria's Catering* in bold blue on the side. As we see in a few minutes, what's arrived is breakfast. Two women, one dressed in white like a chef, hat included, the other in jeans and a red golf shirt, set up a long table on the porch and, within minutes, there are close to 15 dishes warming over small blue flames, the smell of expensive coffee getting all the way over to us. Then this: "I heard from Teddy last month." This is the only other man Helen considered marrying. I offer a non-committal, "No kidding." She says he called out of the blue, then adds that he was just passing through the city. When I stay silent she says he sounded so lost. I ask what he's doing and she tells me he said he was still trying to break into the film business out on the coast. "Says he's finally making some ins." When I ask if he's married yet she says she doesn't know, she didn't ask.

Slowly, most of the party moves to the porch and, sitting with plates on their laps, there's only low conversation and an occasional rattle and tinkling of silverware on china. I glance at Helen to see that some of the light from the party has been caught in her eyes. She looks as young as the first time we met. I feel a jolt from the thought of what would happen to her if our boys were not all right, what would happen to me? For a few seconds there's a terrible fear, but then I force myself to get control and breathe again. Then Helen, her head and eyes just as still as a few minutes ago, asks what Gary and Louis would have had for dinner, and, before she can catch herself, how and where would they ever get to sleep.

Just then I see the colonel, carrying a large tray, come down his steps and over to our porch. He asks, offering the tray with a small gesture, if we'd like some breakfast. He says he saw us a while ago, and that he figured if we were up at this hour something was amiss. As I take the tray and set it down Helen tells him, and he says my God he's sorry and it must be the worst night of our lives. Until right now I haven't thought about it like that, but it strikes a chord in me and I say yes, it is, it sure is. He asks a few general questions, one about where the camp is and if we'll be all right, then says that he hopes the party isn't bothering us. Helen tells him she doesn't know what we'd have done without it. He looks me up and down for a second or two and then, of all things, he asks if I know the date *The Great Gatsby* was published. When I can't instantly bring it to mind, he says 1925. "You teach it, don't you?" he asks. I answer not for some years now. "I read it almost every summer," he says. "Maybe forty times now. A great, great book." Then he turns to look at his house and makes a small sweeping gesture with his right hand. "I think Mr. Gatsby would approve of a party like this," he says. When neither Helen nor I answer he leans forward slightly, just enough to show that he's had more to drink than I first thought, and says, "Wouldn't he?" I answer sure, I'm sure he would, and that brightens his face and he straightens up. "Well," he says, looking first at Helen and then back at me, as if he wishes to say something that will help us, "it's always darkest before the dawn," and then turns and goes carefully down our steps, one hand on the railing. Helen, her voice nearly a whisper, says, "What was that about?" I answer I don't know, say let it go, and look down to the two plates of scrambled eggs with chives, the bacon and muffins. I don't even ask Helen if she wants any.

Just after four the last car from the party leaves, the colonel waving a little like royalty from where he stands on his porch. Out over the ocean the faint arc of first light is just rising, the sky not yet with any real color, dawn more an idea than anything. For the next half hour Helen lies on her side on the wicker sofa, a thin pillow under her head, one hand on the phone right beside her, eyes closed but, I know, not sleeping. One by one the lights in the colonel's house go out and, just before the last one shuts off in their bedroom, I see his silhouette at the open window, one hand on the shade, looking down at us. He stays absolutely still for a long moment, then the shade comes down slowly.

It's not until about a half hour later that the call from Gary comes, and Helen, sitting bolt upright, dumps the phone on the decking. I pick it up and, when I hear his voice, instantly ask if he's all right, if Louis is all right. He says he's fine, but that Louis cut his thumb on a rock climbing a hill. "Man, did it bleed," he says. But he's all right, I ask, and Gary says sure, he himself stopped the bleeding and helped bandage it up. All the time I'm nodding at Helen to tell her everything's okay, and I see her face relax and her eyes fill with relief. Then suddenly I'm angry and ask Gary just what it was that happened that they got lost. Right away he begins to defend the c.i.t. who took them on the hike. He says it wasn't his fault, that they all got confused by an old map that didn't have the two new highways on it. I ignore that and ask if they got any dinner or sleep, and Gary says the sandwiches were gone before dark, and only Louis managed to sleep for about an hour when they gave up and stopped. Then, my eyes on Helen, I tell him we're driving up in a few hours to get them and bring them home. Helen, eyes bright, and her mouth set in a determined line, nods emphatically. "Oh, no," Gary says.

"We're staying." I hear him turn to Louis and confirm this decision with him. Louis says, just loud enough to get to me, "Damn straight."

Then Gary explains that tomorrow is capture-the-flag day, and that the Apaches and the Iroquois—he says they're both Apaches—will be fighting it out all day. I interrupt him by saying we want them both home. "It's best," I say. Again, Helen nods.

"Stay put," Gary says. So emphatic is the statement that for a few seconds I can't believe it came from him. Quietly, in the same voice I've used for years with both of them, I say no, it's been decided. "We are *not*," he says, then for affirmation says, "Right?" to Louis. Another "Damn straight." I hand the phone to Helen and at the same time tell her to talk some sense into them. Helen is even less persuasive than I, and when I see her glance at me several times while saying absolutely nothing I realize Gary's taken over the conversation. Helen says oh, and I see a couple of times and then a really, dear, I didn't know, and, finally, her eyes on me, she turns her free hand palm up and shrugs. Then she covers the mouthpiece with her hand and, both whispering and smiling, says he's telling her about yesterday morning before the hike when the whole camp had the surprise Christmas morning in June and how the whole thing was so fake it was really funny. She looks as if she could listen to him forever. I'm reaching half way across to where Helen is, beckoning for the phone, when I sit back, stopped cold by the memory of when, at five and four, they came into our living room at five fifteen that particular Christmas morning, the bikes ready, training wheels in place since midnight, and how their faces looked, the way they believed.

UPWELLING

Just before seven on this August morning I'm sitting in a rocker on our long wide porch, my bare feet up on the railing, waiting for two things. The first is the wind which will soon come hard out of the southwest, with tiny bits of sand in it, as it has all week, pouring so powerfully across the flat land from the bay to the ocean that upwelling has started, the warm surface water pushed back out to the Gulf Stream, rising in its place the icy bottom currents that come all the way from Labrador. The other is for the trash truck to turn on Madison and start along our street. One of the enduring customs of this town is that in return for its taxes it provides no garbage pickup. Rather, two private companies serve the community, down from three five years ago, and so overburdened are they that no one in the last six years has been added to their routes. Newcomers now have to buy an expensive dump permit and haul their own trash out there. I understand quite well what Mel meant some years ago when he said that in this town you keep the peace with the volunteer fire company and your trash service. The truck comes twice a week, Tuesdays and Fridays, and the five or six men who work our route are so distinctive in appearance that each could be from a different continent. One thing they share, however, is a keen alertness to extra work, which was the problem on Tuesday, two days after Helen and I got here. All day Monday she worked alone, even though I'd offered to help, on the third floor, finally, after all these years, cleaning out and sorting through a great many of Mel's old belongings.

Part of the divorce arrangement between Mel and Mary, just two years before he died, was that she got the house in Wildwood, he the rental in Cape May. His idea was to install central heat and live here year round, but, like a lot of Mel's plans, not much of it got done. In December of that year, having lost the bet that the winter would be mild and he could get by with the gas floor heater in the center hall, he closed the house and took an apartment near the Chalfont, then started seeing a woman named Erma, who'd just been divorced, too. It was a comfortable situation for Mel and that meant he wasn't going to do anything about the house except store everything he owned on the third floor, padlock the door leading up to it, and rent out the other two.

Early Tuesday morning the results of Helen's first efforts were in 22 Hefty bags and six Acme cartons lined up on the strip of grass between the sidewalk and the curb. Through our open bedroom window we heard the truck when it was about half way down our block, the banging of cans and lids, the occasional instruction hollered among the crew as they got nearer. Then clearly, and over the barking of the

Cranemores' Yorkie at the door directly across the street, came the statement, "I ain't no slave labor," followed almost instantly by the truck's gears whining into high. After a moment, in a voice still close to sleep, Helen said, "I am no longer for world peace."

As the wind rises in response to the first hard sunlight on the street, I think that this has not been a good week at all. First, the only reason we're here is that one of our long-time summer tenants, a dentist from Paoli, had a death in the family in California and asked to be let out of the lease. We were at home in Metuchen, our sons on a two-week back-packing trip with our next-door neighbors, planning to refinish the living room floor, when Helen suddenly changed her mind about the realtor's offer to put weekly rentals into the house and called her back to cancel. With the kinds of jobs we have we could have used the money. "We won't break even on the place this year," I said.

"Shoebees," she answered. "Not me."

The last time I'd heard that word Mel and I were rebuilding the front steps, the middle of the porch up on two stacks of cinder blocks. Kneeling, he turned at the sound of the bell from the open-trolley tour and watched it go by. Shoebees, he explained, were day-trippers years ago when the trains ran from Philadelphia, who came down with their lunches in shoeboxes and never spent a nickel in the town. Over time it's come to mean people who stay briefly, a weekend at a bed-and-breakfast or, at most, a week's rental in a house like ours.

I asked Helen what we'd do with the house and without hesitation she said, her eyes out through the large bay window, "Go there until the boys get back." It wasn't until I made a weak gesture to indicate the work we'd leave that I realized she'd already made another decision. "It's time I did the third floor," she said.

The work has been more than Helen thought. The room is huge: half attic, half unfinished living space, with severely sloping eaves on three sides, dormer windows, two ten-foot narrow closets along the back wall, the chimney, with an inch-thick ring of grout dust on the floor around it, in the middle. So crowded was the place when we first looked at it years ago after Mel's funeral that we had to shuffle sideways among the trunks, boxes, piles of old paintings, mostly water colors of beach scenes before the motels went up, stiff plastic clothes carriers that hung from nailed-up poles, old vacuum cleaners, wrought iron and wicker porch furniture and on and on.

Tuesday morning Helen began to divide the things that were left upstairs between Maureen and herself. That took the better part of the day, and when she finished she said, "It's as fair as I can make it." Those were the same words she used that evening when she phoned to tell Maureen what she'd done and to ask when she could drive down and take home her half of Mel's things. Maureen's answer, Helen told me later here on the porch, was, "'What would I want all that old junk for?'" Across her lap was an old photo album she'd found in one of the trunks. "I said, 'Because it's *daddy's*,'" Helen went on, her eyes straight ahead and a little wide. She turned her hands over on the end of the wide flat arms, fingers spread. "And then you know what she said? 'But it's still junk,' that's what." She glanced at me, but only for a second or two, then looked back to the street. "You know what she's got of his?" she asked. I looked over at her. "That Rotary picture's all. Probably the only time he wore a tie." The photograph sits on Maureen's mantle staring straight down their long living room. It doesn't look anything like Mel. Then Helen turned to me and asked, clearly not quite finished with Maureen, "Do you think it's junk?"

"Some of it," I answered.

"Like what?" she asked slowly, her voice rising.

"The box of shoes," I told her, referring to the old Allied carton that must have had 20 different pairs in it, from laced-together work boots with torn soles to shiny tasseled loafers, now cracked, I'd never seen him wear. "And the seascapes."

"He painted those," she said.

"Mel's Blue Period," I answered.

"They're still his," she said, glanced at me again, and then set her eyes hard across the street.

I reached over and without saying anything took the album. Its cover was layered in grit and dust, and the four photographs on the first pages, all beach scenes, must have been at least 40 years old, rectangular Polaroids on which the setting gel had finally cracked and turned light brown. Very quickly I began to recognize, as though coming out of a mist, Mel and Mary in their twenties, he all thin arms and legs in swimming trunks nearly to his knees, she in a one-piece white bathing suit, thin enough that her hip bones showed clearly, and a white cap with a dangling chin strap. They stood holding hands, staring at the camera, self-conscious and shy.

Then there was the accident yesterday morning while Helen and I were eating breakfast out here. The *Star and Wave* van, right on time, came down the street, suddenly went up on its inside wheels for 30 yards or so, and then just as it started to flip over it hit the Cranemores' Ford Escort, righted itself and spun around so hard and fast that its rear and side doors flew open and newspapers went everywhere in the wind. The driver, a short thin black man in his early

20s, jumped down from the van and stood, absolutely fine, one hand pressed to his forehead, staring at where the van had smashed in the top and side of the Escort. Helen and I hurried down the stairs and went over to him. Billie Cranemore, in a long pink robe, flew out the front door and raced across the lawn into the street to stand, as helpless as we, staring at the car. Without looking at the black man, her eyes staring at the crushed side of the car, she quietly said that Blake was calling the police. Then the black man sat down in the space where one of the side doors was thrown open, put his face in his hands, and began to cry. His upper body rocked slowly as over and over he said, "My first day."

Then Blake came running across the lawn to the car. One glance told him it was totaled. His arms rose to waist-high and then slapped down against his sides. "Jack," he said to me, "this is a bad dream." Within a few minutes a police car showed up, lights flashing, but no siren, and about five minutes later the tow truck came slowly down Madison and turned onto New York. The cop was as nice to the black man as he could be, helped him up, put an arm around him, then shook his head at Billie when she said, pointing, that he was going to get his ass sued off. The black man, now remarkably composed after crying so hard, told the cop as honestly as he could that something went wrong with the steering, that all of a sudden it was soft in his hands and the van went hard and crazy to the right. The cop asked him a couple of questions, found out he lived in North Cape May, saw his license, asked if Obie Crane were his mother, then, just as he said things'd be all right, the black man began to shake all over, repeated to everyone that it was his first day, and sat down once more. Within a few seconds he was again crying hard, actually sobbing, as if he'd found the only way he could rid himself of the terror, fear and sorrow of it all.

The cop looked down at him, patted his shoulder, and said, "Go ahead, go ahead." Then after a moment he added, "You could have been killed."

In all of this I did not notice that Helen had silently gone back to the porch where, when I finally turned around, I saw her on the top step leaning against one of the columns, watching the black man. She looked like an old photograph where it's hard to make out the person's face.

We didn't talk about the accident until later that evening on Philadelphia beach. The wind had picked up and with the sun just down it was actually a little cold close to the water. Helen brought up the morning by saying that someone she'd known in college had gone to England on a Fulbright and her first day there checked the traffic the wrong way, stepped off the curb, and died instantly. When I asked her what she did about it she said that when she heard the news she went to her room, locked the door, and cried like hell.

After a few more minutes we got to the first of the huge black rocks of the jetty. Helen put a hand on my shoulder and slipped off her sandals and set them on the rocks, then turned and waded into the water, stood for a few moments and stepped back, the tops of her feet white from the cold. Then she climbed onto the first rock and stood almost three feet above me. She stepped onto the next one, so wet and shiny it looked icy, then quickly with a series of light leaps she was out where the deep water began. As I went toward her she turned away and stared at the horizon, her hands in her pockets, back stiff. The round ghost of the moon was already up, to the right of it faint points of light from the first couple of stars. I stood a few feet behind her. She turned a little so I could see the side of her face. Her chin was raised slightly, her eyes far in the distance. Around us the water had some small degree of red in it.

"You'd get rid of everything, I suppose," she said.

"I'd keep that photo album," I answered.

"I put it in the car," she said. "And?" I shook my head and she looked away again. "Between you and Maureen," she said.

"Why do you still miss him so?" I asked.

Her voice flat and gone away somewhere, she said, "Sometimes in the kitchen when no one's home I'll just go ahead and let it all out."

"Which is why you wanted to come down here," I said. She nodded, then said she thought that somehow doing the third floor would be good for her. "But even with all that stuff piled by the curb," she said, "I still sit up there and cry."

It was then that we both noticed the darkness coming on fast, the beach and half the jetty only long, flat shadows at right angles, the soft neon from the motels taking over. We started back over the rocks, Helen first, the surfaces even more dangerous than when we'd come out, the wind worse. When we got to the beach I jumped down first, and, together, we picked up our shoes from the rock and began to walk in the shallow, icy water. After the first shot of pain there was a surprising calmness to it.

About half way up the beach she said, "Your mother once told me that at your father's funeral she 'shed not a tear.'"

"His drinking caused a lot of pain," I told her. "She still writes him letters in her head telling him off," I added. "After all these years, too."

"And she said you didn't cry, either."

"But a week later I sure did," I said, then told her my brother Phil and I were at a Pirates game. "I hadn't even thought about the funeral," I said.

"You cried at a baseball game?"

I laughed a little and then said, "Phil kept telling me to shut the hell up and what the hell was wrong with me anyway." The sand moved like dry snow under our feet, but there was no sound.

"In front of all those people?" she said, shook her head and then turned away to look up toward the boardwalk and the huge old houses along Beach Avenue, each porch and every window full of light. "I couldn't do that," she said.

"I was seventeen," I told her. "What did I know?" Then, after a moment, I said, "Is that why you walked away this morning?"

"When you feel like that it ought to be private," she said. Way up ahead the lights from Convention Hall made it look like a ship in the night. "He just lost it," she said.

"That he did," I answered.

"Nobody can help you, you know," she said. "Not when you feel like that."

"It's all yours," I said. "That's for sure."

We did not talk until we got up on the boardwalk and started down toward Convention Hall and the arcade, the wind, now that we were out of the protection of the beach, hard enough to make us turn our heads. The lights from the arcade, fudge and taffy shops next to Convention Hall, where there was the usual Thursday evening sing-a-long of old show tunes, made it feel as if these were the last few hours of a pleasant, unnamed holiday.

We stopped in front of the arcade, its huge windows, harsh lights and loud music making it seem like an odd bubble of pleasure floating in the night. Computer and video games hummed and sang, young boys absorbed by them, dime poker machines flashed randomly, older people hunched before them, and in front of the row of skeeball games all along one wall teenagers and adults rolled wooden balls at the targets, the scoring bells incessant. In the middle of the arcade was the change booth, raised a couple of feet or so and made to look like an oldtime bank teller's cage. In it was a hugely fat middle-aged woman whose face looked to have the gift of perfect skin. In her eyes, though, was a locked sadness, as if she knew that what she felt was hers alone forever. She slid tokens and change back and forth under the bars as though practicing on some silent musical keyboard.

Just as a particularly unpleasant gust of wind, with what felt like a handful of sand sprinkled through it, whipped along the boardwalk, I turned to Helen to ask if she wanted to go back to the house. She was staring intently through the glass to where, in front of the last of the skeeball games, the black man who'd had the accident held two wooden balls, his concentration on the target obvious. Next to him, her hand over her mouth to suppress a laugh, stood a pregnant woman his own age.

He rolled the first ball, watched it pop into the air and land in the outer ring. He glanced at the woman and she openly giggled at him. The second went straight into the bull's-eye and the scoreboard on the top of the game lit up and flashed different colors. From where we were we could not hear the bells ring. Like a child, his face full of delight, he raised both arms above his head and shook them.

Helen watched him for a while, her hands on the glass, her face close to it. She seemed perplexed, even slightly irritated, her expression one that said that if he were closer to her she might very well demand of him why he thought he had a right to his pleasant, even serene, state of mind. She watched without moving, except for bringing her hands up beside her face to cut the glare, while he rolled the last two wooden balls, both bull's-eyes. Then he and the young woman moved away, he with his arm across her shoulders, and disappeared behind the change booth and a wall of computer games in the back.

After a long moment we walked away, neither of us looking back, toward Convention Hall. Helen was sullen and drawn into herself and only when we passed one of the young girls standing outside Morrow's Fudge Shop with her box of samples, toothpicks standing in each small square, did Helen seem to brighten. The girl smiled at Helen and raised the box slightly. Helen took two pieces, each not more than a half inch square, and handed me one.

Together, we ate the fudge, its sweet freshness a small wondrous explosion in the mouth, the aftertaste something that seemed as though it might linger forever. I put a hand on Helen's shoulder and asked if she wanted to split a quarter of a pound. When she hesitated I said, "Come on, two pieces each." Her answer was to shake her head vaguely, as though she really hadn't tasted the fudge, and then turn away toward Convention Hall where just inside its wide open front doors the voices of at least a hundred people suddenly started in on, "Oh, What a Beautiful Morning." Helen stood for a long few moments listening. She looked as though she had never heard the song.

The trash truck slowly turns the corner far up the block, two men hanging off each side by one arm, as if they are school kids, another walking by the driver's door, looking up and gesturing with both arms, two more some twenty yards back, already moving from behind the truck to the first of the houses where, either late last night or very early this morning, the cans were set by the curb.

When we got back from the boardwalk last night Helen

had decided, sometime during our walk, that the rest of Mel's things from the third floor would go out with the trash this morning, except, she said, anything that I might want.

Together, we went through what was left up there, and I took two rakes and then, together, we brought down the two large cartons that contained his complete set of Dickens. On the way to the car I saw that the teeth on the bamboo leaf rake were split, its wires broken, and I tossed it onto the pile of things at the curb.

The small steel rake I put across the floor of the back seat of the car. The head of it would be just right for working the small spaces in our garden at home. The books went into the trunk to either side of the photo album. I offered to help Helen bring down the rest of the stuff, but she said it was something she wanted to do by herself.

She worked until well after midnight and then both of us were up this morning just after six to bring down the last of the things, a coat rack that used to stand in the front hall of their home in Wildwood, one of its prongs snapped off years ago, a box of dishes that held some old coffee cups she remembered from that place, too, as well as some of the old plates and silverware he furnished this house with.

There were other things, about five trips' worth, which while I've been sitting here she's marched down the front steps and out to the curb all by herself. She now draws my attention to the two bundles of Mel's seascapes, and she has a joke about them as she stops on the top step. "Mel did an amazing number of things," she says, raising the bundle in her right arm. "Most poorly."

I want to respond to her, to tell her something comforting, even sentimental, perhaps remind her again how close we all were back then. But she turns away as if I'm not even there and goes down the steps and out to the curb.

She stands, holding the paintings, looking up the street to where the trash truck slowly comes along. In situations like this Helen is an expert, and I have to remind myself that if I want the men to take everything away I should stay where I am, I should sit still. Helen is a peacemaker who will not mention Tuesday morning, and she will get done what she's there for.

The truck arrives before the men, and the driver, an elbow out his window, has a pleasant enough smile. He tells Helen that the company will have to make an additional charge for so large a pickup. He doesn't wait for her to answer but, instead, shows her a clipboard and writes something down. Helen picks up the first of the bags, one in each hand, and heaves both together into the back of the truck.

One by one the men catch up to the truck and silently, shamed it seems by her efforts, begin to toss bag after bag into the back. One of the men, the smallest but certainly not the weakest, stacks two of the cartons of Mel's stuff and lifts both with ease. From where I am I get several glances from the men which contain the clear message that they think she ought to be up here, I down there.

I rise and go to the top step, then stop. Because Helen has her back to the men and is just bending over to get two more bags I am the first to see that she is crying. I realize that because her actions are routine and repetitive, the men, even when she takes the few steps to the back of the truck, have not yet noticed. What stops me from going down now is how openly she sobs, her upper body in small heaves even as she lugs two more bags over to the truck. Clearly, she does not care who sees her.

Slowly, the men become aware of her crying and stop and look at her. I move away from the steps and come back to the rocker and sit down. The men become quite still in front of her while she goes back and forth from the curb. One by one, then, each turns his head up to where I am. They look at me as if they think I'm crazy, as if they think I don't know what I'm doing.

A MESSAGE FROM MEL

It's the first Sunday in June here and I'm painting a window in one of the front bedrooms on the second floor of this old house we've had now for fourteen years, ever since Mel died and left it to us. This morning the ocean moves like an animal able to express anger only through its shoulders, the clouds are gray and thick over the flat motels two blocks up on Beach Avenue, and I know even before the D.J. on the country station out in the hall says it that a storm is moving up the coast. This time of year the sky is usually a smooth, washed-out blue with great highways of arching, thin clouds, not, as it is now, as wet and cold as late March. What's on the way is no hurricane—the real storm's a hundred miles southeast—but the D.J. has rightly warned of strong winds and coastal flooding.

After a few seconds of silence from the radio I stop in mid-stroke on the sill thinking it's another brief power failure like there've been since I got here Thursday. Then the D.J. says in a flat, honest voice, "Good friends, I have bad news." He pauses and then very slowly says, "We have lost Conway." As he gives the details of how Twitty was found in his bus, the transport to the hospital, the failure of the surgery, his voice is all but gone.

Then the rising wind against the ageless panes makes a cool breath on my hand and I remember that eleven years ago it was only because Helen had promised her father that we'd paint the downstairs woodwork, in exchange for a week here, that I was alone in the house when the call came from Maureen in Red Bank that Mel had died suddenly. Instantly, I had two thoughts, both absurd: why had the news traveled up the Jersey coast and back when Mel had died only six blocks away; and the conversation on the beach the day before, he cross-legged in the bright sun, Helen nursing Gary under the umbrella, I on my back off to the side, her old straw hat over my face, in which each tried to pay for the paint. From under the brim I could see the identical slope of their shoulders, the same bumps in their cervical spines. His tan swimming trunks were still dark from the water, and his thick black hair, that only in the last year had finally gotten some white into it, was flat and straight. He and Helen compromised. "You buy the brushes," he said.

"And the masking tape," she answered.

From under Helen's hat I watched Mel stare hard at the baby, flushed from the sun and the breast, squirming complacently for sleep on Helen's chest. Mel's eyes were sharp and full of yearning, his lips parted so slightly that it seemed in one instant he'd both thought of something important to say and abandoned it. His gaze slowly covered Helen, his expression that of wonder, even amazement, at her presence. Then he turned his head away to look at the water and the children playing at its edge, then farther out toward the thin, perfect horizon.

My mind now searches the house for Mel. The tiny downstairs bathroom flashes by, a place we re-did together, a room so small that often his hand was on my shoulder or my knee was braced against his side. Then he is at work on the two windows on the front porch that have the inset of stained glass at the top, which he restored himself, then replacing the front steps, hauling the new washer and dryer up from the basement during the flooding two years before, the time he said, smiling, that he didn't know why he'd ever become a lawyer when old houses were what he really loved. All of it goes by in a flash.

During the afternoon callers to the radio station mourn, and Conway Twitty songs are played so often that by early evening when I bike through the light rain down to the Ugly Mug for something to eat, as I have each night, I know the lyrics of several. I take Beach Avenue by the ocean to get a look at the tide, and I see that already the water has covered the beach right up to the boulders at the base of the boardwalk. Now and again one of the waves slams into the huge rocks and sends up a white and blue spray that settles at my feet.

At home in Metuchen all that's left of him is an album of old photos of Mary and him, his complete Dickens, and some yard tools. But as I turn away from the ocean and start up Decatur Street toward the warm lights of the bars and shops it feels as if he is everywhere: the silhouette just closing the front door of a bed-and-breakfast up the way, the shadow in the old pickup turning into the parking lot by the Pilot House restaurant, even the man in the sweatshirt and Phillies cap sitting in a rocker on the old porch of a private house, eyes out on what he can see of the ocean through the rain.

The Mug is almost empty, the shoebees gone early to beat the storm, and only four people sit at the huge, oval bar: two young men at the end, who I've seen roofing, and an older, pleasant-looking couple two stools away, she in a navy-blue windbreaker, he a sedate maroon blazer, a folded raincoat on the bar next to him.

Tommy Ben puts a Lite and a coaster in front of me and when he asks why I'm trying to do all four upstairs rooms in a week I tell him because they're suddenly peeling like crazy and we've got the summer tenants coming in a couple of weeks. Then I add, as though someone else says it, just how long it's been. He gives a short, soft whistle as he sets a menu next to the beer and says it's a miracle the paint lasted so long in the salt air. "It was all in the preparation," I answer quickly. "My father-in-law did it." Then when I add, "Mel," as if that word alone is all that's needed to explain the high quality of the work, the woman turns and asks me if I mean Mel Landry. Surprised, I stare at her for a moment. Certainly she is fifteen years older than I, perhaps late fifties or a little more, but her face, round with soft, dark eyes, seems without age. When she sees I'm trying to place her she says her name, Erma, and, when that gets no response, "The funeral." Vaguely she and that hard, confusing time return, Mel separated from Mary for two years, he living on and off with Erma, each wanting the place of prominence at his service, Erma the loser. "I remember your last name was Henderson," she says. The round red face of the man next to her suddenly appears over her shoulder, then he tips back to get a good look at me and I see his Century 21 nameplate on the lapel pocket. "Jack," I say and she closes her eyes briefly, as if in further recognition, and then he says, "Bill," and gives a small salute. He raises a glass of dark beer. There is the sense about him that he is an extremely likeable man, and for a long moment I concentrate more on him than her. Then Erma says she remembers Helen and that she'd just had a baby, and I nod and tell her we've got two boys now. She holds her eyes steadily on me, the kind of look that if it were from a woman I was close to would mean that somehow I'd hurt her. She breaks it off and says Bill's her husband.

"Nine years now," Bill says, then follows it quickly with, "And where're you from?"

The word, *Metuchen,* is in my mind, but I don't say it. Instead, as if with some other, cleaner voice, I tell him I'm originally from Pennsylvania, and when he asks exactly where I say the middle of the state.

"You hunt?" he asks, his head perfectly still, his eyes absolutely clear.

"Not anymore," I say. I glance at Erma and see that she is looking at me as if she hears none of the conversation. Bill asks why and I tell him, my voice flat and honest, that my father died while he was hunting.

"Accident?" he asks.

"Heart," I tell him. "Sitting under a tree, the rifle across his knees." Then I add, not knowing where it comes from, "And drunk."

"Gone just like Mel," Erma says.

"Except Mel was no alky," I tell her, surprised at the hardness in my voice. "He wasn't a *bum*," I add, again feeling how involuntarily it comes.

Erma then asks if I'm still a teacher and I tell her yes and she nods and smiles and says Mel used to brag that I'd read everything under the sun.

"Real estate runs in my family," Bill says. He tips back

again so I can see him. "Your old man teach, too?"

"Industrial arts," I answer. "Woodshop. And back before all the machines." I say it with pride. I remember then, hard and suddenly, like the sting from a highway pebble, the bookcase he made for me at 11, the perfect dove-tailing, the miter joints as smooth as eyelids. And I remember helping him, too, when he paneled our basement and moved the television and some old chairs down there, even the very day he told me the reason I couldn't measure anything right, or shoot a rifle properly, was because I sight with the wrong eye.

"Where's your house?" Bill asks, and when I answer it's on New York Avenue his eyebrows snap up and he says, "Location, location." Erma smiles at this and then Bill says, "Know what it's worth?"

I tell him I haven't any idea, then look at Erma. "Mel got it for a song," I say proudly. Then Bill asks me if I want to sell it, an idea that nearly overpowers me. "No," I say and smile at him, "not at all." As if he simply hasn't heard me he says that a lot's happened to the market in the last few years and asks if he can do a walk-through tomorrow and give me a figure. I tell him that he can if he wants but that he's wasting his time. He says, smiling, not if he gets the listing if we ever sell. Just then the front door of the bar swings wide from a powerful gust of wind, and each of us turns to look out at the storm and how gusts of rain sweep up into the street light. Then one of the roofers near the front gets off his stool and closes the door. "Just when they get the new beach in," Bill says, his reference to the months of dredging and reclamation that've gone on to repair all the years of storm damage.

As if all along Erma has been thinking of something else, she says quietly, "Mel could be a bastard when he wanted." I say, protectively, that he sure had a blunt way with some things. "But the sun rose and set on his kids," she says. "And you, too."

Then without warning they are both leaving, as though between them some signal I couldn't see has passed. Erma slides off the stool, both hands on the zipper of the windbreaker, and Bill struggles into his raincoat. Erma takes a couple of small steps toward me and we shake hands, mine in both of hers. She says it was nice to meet me again, and I tell her the same, and then she says she's sorry they've got to leave but the tidal flooding down by the bridge might close it. On the stool Bill looked to be as tall as Mel, certainly as powerful looking through the shoulders and head, but now, standing, I'm surprised that he's almost half a foot shorter. "A.M. tomorrow," he says as he reaches past Erma and shakes my hand. "Come hell or high water." He thinks this is funny and laughs and, dutifully, Erma rolls her eyes in a way both tolerant and intimate. My response is to say again that they're welcome to come by, but the house is probably never going to be on the market.

By the middle of the morning, when I am again painting, I see out the window that the clouds are still a heavy gray, the rain in fat lazy mists along the street. Far out to sea the real storm seems to rest along the horizon like a soft black wish. I have two memories of a sky like this: one the year Helen and I were married and Mel gave us this house for the week after Labor Day; the other at 12 waiting most of an afternoon for my father in this kind of rain outside the wrong bar.

Through the window I see a white pickup come slowly down our street, its parking lights on so that it looks a little sleepy. I turn away to glance at the ocean, the storm like a planned confusion of silence, and then I look back to see the pickup veer slightly and stop by the curb directly across from the house. Erma gets out the driver's side, Bill from the other door, clipboard in hand. It strikes me as wholly appropriate that Erma would have just such a truck, a Chevy three-quarter ton, the kind, if he were still alive, Mel would insist on. For several long moments they stand in the light rain by the truck looking up at the house, now and again pointing at something that interests them.

Bill disappears around the side of the house and I watch Erma, all alone, lean back against the door of the pickup, arms crossed, one foot over the other at the ankles. Her eyes move over the porch and the downstairs windows, then briefly up to where I'm standing. I raise a hand but immediately realize that with the low-level glare from the clouds she can't see me. I watch her carefully then, and for a few moments I'm certain she's thinking about Mel, perhaps even a time or two when she might have helped him out in the house. Maybe, I think, it was actually she who chose the new crockery back then or bought the green and white towels that went so well with the new bedspreads. When Bill reappears from the other side of the house Erma shoves off from the pickup to cross the street, and, together, they approach the porch steps. Bill, I see, doesn't miss anything. In a way I do not expect, he reminds me of how Mel took in everything, and how, in fact, in a lot we did together he was way ahead of me.

"You're welcome to look around," I say at the door, smiling, proud of the place. As Bill disappears into the back by the kitchen I see Erma first look up at the high ceilings, then into the two front rooms, and finally she walks over and looks carefully at the old oak facing on the side of the staircase. Then she goes left into the dining room and stares up at the glass-tasseled chandelier Mel and I put up the year before he died. I'm waiting for a compliment on it, and when none comes I say, "Mel picked it out."

"That I believe," she says.

Bill goes from the kitchen into the hall and starts up the stairs, his feet heavy enough on the bare wood that the tassels on the chandelier tremble but do not touch. Erma turns abruptly and goes into the kitchen, glances around, says, "Nice floor," to which I respond that I laid the linoleum myself, and then she steps past me and back into the hall. When she stops at the stairs and looks up like she's waiting to hear exactly where Bill's gotten to she asks me what's up there. I tell her four bedrooms and a bath, then to the surprised look on my face she says, "I was never in this place." She runs her hand along the banister, then looks at the risers and the way they've been kicked over the years. I see that the steps have smooth, shallow places in them from all the tenants and their kids and that once again they need at least a fine sanding and more stain. Erma reaches out and touches the wood, then rubs her fingers together. "What this place could stand," she says, "is a good carpenter." Two things happen to me then. One is that I have a brief, imperfect flash of my father working here, an unfair and unwanted intrusion of memory, and the other is that I come instantly to Mel's defense and tell Erma that Mel did fine work on his houses. "True," she says. "For a handyman." I suppress an urge to argue with her and nod and smile. Then I realize I am hurt by how she has devalued him, and I want to let her know how close I was to him. With Bill going from room to room upstairs there is a moment I take advantage of.

"I often wonder," I say, "why you two never got

married."

"It was my fault," she answers.

From what I know I piece together instantly that what she's telling me isn't right. In my mind is Mel's answer, given a month before he died, when he told me, almost laughing, that as far as Erma was concerned he just wasn't ready for that much love. I expect now to hear it was she who would not commit to him, that she'll offer a rationalization that over the years has become a personal truth. Then she says, "Mine, all right." She turns and looks straight at me. "I would have given anything to have married him," she says. "He was the dearest, nicest man." I smile and nod, pleased that she's so honest, pleased that we feel the same way. "But I was on the rebound then," she says, "and it was Mel who knew it wouldn't work." She turns slightly to look out again at the still lowering clouds, then smiles and her eyes come back to me. "He was special," she says, then turns away as Bill starts down the stairs.

"This place sure needs a lot of work," he says, his head down, writing.

"But I've kept it up," I manage, defensive, even a little angry.

His response is to free the paper from the clipboard and hand it to me. "As best you could, sure," he says. "It's just what time does." He smiles.

"I'm not going to sell," I tell him. "Things are okay the way they are." His answer is that that's true so long as I want to stay in the rental business. "But major renovations if it ever goes on the market," he adds.

I glance at Erma who has turned away and is now looking back into the dining room, first at the chandelier, then with a slow swivel to the kitchen and hallway. She seems to be looking for Mel, or, I think, at least some sign of him, something old, just a kind of presence. Then as abruptly as they left The Mug last night Bill silently shakes my hand and turns for the door. Erma, sensing his leaving, follows without looking at him.

Outside, on the porch, Bill says he'll do a couple of comparables just to get a hard figure and when I say that isn't necessary, he answers he's got the time, the first part of June is always slow. Just as Bill turns slightly and gives me one of his small salutes, Erma says, "And with a family, you should know the value of things." Then they go down the steps and I watch them hurry across the street through the rain, wait for her to raise a hand from the other side of the pickup, which she does not, and then my eyes carefully follow the truck as it goes all alone down the street and turns the corner to go up to Beach Avenue. Then another clear memory of my father comes, as though directly from the center of that storm, in which he said, just once, through his turpentine breath, "Oh, how I love you so."

THREE'S A CROWD

Right now Helen and I are in The Pilot House restaurant, having just biked down from the house. We're at a table near the fireplace on this gray March evening, the logs already melting into large orange coals. Helen's cheeks are red from the ride and mine feel the same way, too. Just after we order— flounder for her and stuffed shrimp for me—and two white wines come, she quietly says, as if it's been a part of a very long conversation, "Teddy called Wednesday." I have no trouble remembering that it's been just about five years since he last called. "'Just to say hello,'" she said then. I say nothing. "He's in New York and, well..." she goes on, then turns her right hand palm up.

"Really?" I manage. Then, in the same tone, I say, pretty much without thinking, "What's he up to?" Helen's eyes have already shifted to the fireplace and the coals that seem as if they will shimmer endlessly. As though I should know all about the film business, she says, "'...from L.A. for some establishing shots.' For a t.v. film he's directing," she adds.

"Oh?" I say. Then she asks if I know that most of the t.v. stuff set in New York is actually shot in L.A. "He's married now?" I try, and Helen shakes her head slowly, then smiles as she says he's got a house with a heart-shaped pool and two Dalmatians. "His third film," she adds.

"I see."

"He's been all over," she goes on. Briefly, she looks my way and then back to the fire. She ticks off Mexico, "southern France several times," Thailand and, she finishes, "'even,' he said, 'a stint in the sub-Sahara.'"

"Very glamorous," I say as our house salads arrive. If she hears my tone it makes no impression. She picks up her fork and sends the tines straight into the middle of a plump cherry tomato, twists it to get a good coating of balsamic on it, then eats it. "Life with Teddy would have been different," I say. What of course I want is for her to say something reassuring, that she sure is glad after all's said and done that she married me. Instead, she says, "I know."

As she goes after the other cherry tomato, I ask, "And what does one talk about to an old love?" She smiles a little, but does not look at me. Slowly, she chews the tomato, obviously pleased with its taste. "Mostly," she finally says, "the boys. He wanted to know all about them." Briefly, I think of them and wonder how they're getting along for the weekend at Maureen's.

Then I say, "For my money, he's just checking up on your marriage."

"Yes, I suppose he is," she says. Now she spears a large ring of red onion and, after a bit of maneuvering, gets it into her mouth. The taste of this pleases her, too. Then she looks directly at me for a long time, her eyes all over my face and shoulders, as if in a very frank appraisal.

"Did you tell him you had a good marriage?" I ask.

"It never came up," she answers.

Just then dinner comes and we eat our first few bites silently, each glancing in turn at the fire, its heat still as strong as when we came in. Outside, it's started to rain, Decatur Street slick and black under the street lights. In a way that seems as if it comes at the end of a day dream, Helen asks what I think the rest of our lives will be like. With a small smile I shake my head and say I don't know, we're only in our thirties. Then I hear that what she's just asked has a quiet echo of meaning, a certain lost quality. I glance up and see that her eyes are on the fire, in them the kind of thin water that comes with melancholy. I think then that teaching and library work are pretty dull stuff. "What would you like it to be?" I ask.

"If I knew I'd say," she answers.

Then I'm much too quick to say that everyone's in a rut—at least everyone we know—because it's not out of my mouth for an instant before she says, "Janet Willoughby isn't." Her reference is to the wife of Father Gill, one of the Episcopal priests in our parish: 34 with three kids and she upped and left it all to go back to Oklahoma to live with her high-school sweetheart. Turned out that they'd begun writing while he was doing four years for a D.U.I. homicide. It's been all over the parish for months. "The whole thing just boggles...," I say. Then, again, she's looking away at the fire.

"Do you think Janet's happy?" she asks.

I shrug and say, "Who knows?"

She says that, if I really want the truth, she's sick and tired of the nasty little people in the parish condemning Janet. "Maybe," she says, "she did something brave."

"She hurt four innocent people," I answer.

"Was she supposed to be dishonest, live her life for everyone else?"

"Put that way," I say, "no. It's just that the whole thing seems tragic."

"It is," she says, "but that doesn't make her wrong." Then, as if she's given much more thought to the situation than just this conversation, she says, "She chose between a moral obligation to herself and her family responsibilities."

"Exactly."

"Few women make her kind of decision," she says. Then she reaches for the dessert menus standing on their sides between the salt and pepper shakers.

Outside, the rain has eased into a light drizzle, and when I ask if she wants to take the long way home along Beach Avenue and the boardwalk her answer is to point her bike that way and give a strong shove with one foot. Briefly, I watch her glide away through the cone of a street light and then into the darkness. When I catch up to her at the end of the block she's at the red light in the middle of the empty street, her arms folded, a light glaze from the drizzle on her face, eyes fixed on the ocean just beyond the boardwalk. "I wish I could tell you," she says, "that I didn't like his calling."

The light changes to green and we push off to the other side of Beach Avenue and nose our bikes into the long empty rack. In the summer there are four or five of these, always full. I take my lock and loop it through both front wheels and, with a solid click, close the padlock. Then we go up the ramp and onto the boardwalk. The shops and arcades are closed and, in most cases, gated. We lean on the railing and look down at the waves as they slide around the pilings and then bump against the boulders just below us. Far out there is a single white light near the horizon, either from a dead-slow freighter or, perhaps, a single star through a small break in the clouds. "Do you still have feelings for him?" I ask.

"It was pretty intense back then," she says. Then I tell her that the last night she saw him when she turned him down—the night I kept calling and calling—I nearly drank myself out of my mind. She tells me she didn't know that, that when she finally called around midnight all my roommate said was that I'd gone to bed. "On the floor," I tell her.

"I did think you were awfully calm about it all," she says.

"Just flat missed the bed."

She raises her head and looks out toward the ocean, the sky and water so black that they are inseparable. "What I remember most," she says—really, it sounds as if it's to herself—"was how he loved to dance." For the moment, I'm not even there. "I did love him," she says. She turns toward me but does not look at me.

Just as we come in the front door, and even before Helen turns on the hall light, we both smell it: Major, the McCarthy's cat from next door, has—for the third time in the last year—gotten into our house through the half-broken ground-level window in the basement, and taken, pun intended, a major dump right in the middle of the living room floor. I hit the light and, together, we stare at it. Helen asks why that little bastard would do such a thing, and I tell her I haven't the faintest idea. Together, with lots of paper towels, the rubber gloves and a dustpan from the basement, and the big jug of Fantastik, we start to clean it up. Helen is not happy that the sloppy duct-tape-and-cardboard repair job I did last fall has clearly failed, and she makes me promise that before we leave Sunday that window will finally be f-i-x-e-d.

A while later I'm in the kitchen tying up the ends of the garbage bag when the phone rings in the hallway and Helen answers it. I go still for a moment thinking that it's the boys calling or, more probably, Maureen with the day's news about them. It's Teddy. I know this from how Helen says, surprised, "Oh, how are you?" While I listen I place the yellow plastic tie around the neck of the bag and pull it as tight as I can. Pleasantries out of the way, Teddy gets down to business. I become aware that I'm like a large awkward statue caught in the process of trying to stand up—and so, slowly, I do, and it's then I realize the extent to which my heart's racing.

Then the picture of Helen and Teddy—the only time I ever met him—comes into my mind: the two of them walking across the Columbia campus, he with an arm around her shoulders, she glancing up at him adoringly, he, yes, in a varsity letter sweater with a big *C* on his chest. They stopped by my bench where I was trying to read *Ulysses* for the third time. Helen and I had been out a few times—coffee, a Japanese film I couldn't understand at all, and a stuffy department tea. Teddy's handshake was apelike, his smile a toothpaste ad, his demeanor forceful and, as I confessed to her later, wholly intimidating. "Oh, yes," he managed from behind his huge, perfect teeth, "Helen *did* mention you." He was, frankly, the kind of guy you'd like to punch in the nose, but, at the same time, you knew that if you did you'd get the worst of it. Right then, his arm still around Helen's shoulders, he gave a little squeeze and pulled her into him, looked down at her, and said, "The high-school teacher, right?"

"Teddy wants to make movies," Helen said, trying to lighten the moment. She tried, or, at least I think I saw her try, to move away from him a little. Then, with a disdain I'd never experienced, he looked me over and asked what fraternity I'd been in. I gave him the two-fold answer that I'd been in none and had gone to Rutgers.

Suddenly, Helen's standing in the kitchen doorway, eyes red, arms crossed. She more or less slumps against the door jamb, then says that the call was from Teddy and, if it were all right with everybody, he'd like to come down tomorrow. My reaction is to tell her that I'm not so sure it is, and why does he want to see you after all these years? "You're married with two kids," I say. Helen, her expression calm, as if she expected exactly what I said and was only waiting to get it out of the way, answers, "Teddy's dying."

Over the next several minutes Helen tells me that Teddy's not filming anything, he's been at New York Hospital for the last two weeks and that what he's got in the right side of his brain is, "'Well,' he said, 'unpleasant.'"

"And he wants to come here?" I say, my tone as though I'm trying to verify something I can't quite believe. "Tomorrow?"

We look at each other for a long moment, then I break it off, pick up the garbage bag, and start out the door. When she says, "Seeing him is something I have to do," I answer, "Okay, okay."

When Teddy arrives Saturday afternoon just before one, it's with quite a flare: BMW convertible, top down, somewhat defiantly, I think, since it's only in the high

50s with hard low clouds out over the ocean. I see the car go right by the house, Teddy looking first left then right, then left again, checking numbers, and when he does a hard *U* half a block down and comes slowly back I get a good look at him. Astonishingly, he appears no different at all than when I last saw him—except for the letter sweater—replaced now by a dark green windbreaker, the kind of guy, I let myself think, who's always going to look young. As he gets out and looks up at the house I have the thought that there's nothing wrong with him at all, the whole thing's a ruse. But just as I call to Helen back in the kitchen that he's here I see him reach into the small space behind the bucket seats and lift out a cane. His left side unsteady, he comes around the front of the car and, with some additional effort, over the curb.

Helen takes only a brief look over my shoulder through the living room window before she goes straight out the front door and quickly down the steps. I'm not surprised that they embrace, but I don't much like it when it seems to me to go on for too long, Teddy's cane off the ground, both arms around Helen. By the time I get through the front door and to the top of our steps they've broken it off, but Helen is still holding onto his right arm as they start toward me. "Hey, there, Jack," Teddy says almost musically, now more weight on the cane than I'd seen. I say hi back and that I'm glad you could come, but as they start up the stairs neither seems to hear me. I open the screen door as wide as I can and they go in. Helen steers him into the smaller living room to the right where he sits in the middle of the two vinyl-covered cushions on the wicker couch.

For a few minutes he's full of questions about the house: what the summer rates are, taxes, upkeep, commissions. Helen answers him with general numbers, as if the two of them are negotiating something I'm not a part of, don't really even understand, and then Helen changes the subject and asks him if he'd like some lunch. He says yes, he sure would, just no red meat, please. Helen leaves without looking back at either of us, and then Teddy turns to me—I'm standing with my arms folded by the wide door—and says, "Know what this house will be worth in twenty, thirty years?" He answers his own question with, "A lot." Then, finally, our eyes really meet and he says, "She looks absolutely terrific."

During lunch, Helen and Teddy make plans: he wants us all to "zip up to Bali's in Atlantic City for some slots and roulette," then dinner on him. Helen, with a long glance at me, says fine, but first she'd like to drive him around town, out to the Point, show him the marina. I read in Helen's eyes that what I say and do now is important to her. After a long moment I say that you two ought to go it alone, after all three's a crowd, and I've got a basement window to fix before we leave tomorrow. Clearly, from how the mood lightens and conversation picks up—and Teddy tells a couple of very good Hollywood jokes—it was the right thing to say.

As I'm cleaning up in the kitchen while Helen's upstairs getting ready, I suddenly become aware of Teddy standing in the doorway leaning on his cane. "I'm not going to get mushy about it," he says, "but thanks." For this I really have no words. Holding the chicken-salad bowl, I look at him, then nod, as if this will tell him I understand. Then, with his huge smile, he turns and starts to walk down the hall. Even with his cane each step seems more precarious than the one before and halfway to the front door he puts out his right arm to steady himself against the wall.

A few minutes later I'm standing by the kitchen doorway when Helen comes down and the two of them start toward the front door without so much as a goodbye in my direction. I say I hope you have a good time and she looks back at me, blows a kiss, and says, "There's ground beef in the fridge," and then is out the door. I stand absolutely still for several minutes until I hear the car start up and, finally, drive off. Amazingly, then, in the doorway that leads from the kitchen down to the basement, Major appears. He doesn't see me right away, his head in a cunning little swivel, and I wait until he comes out into the middle of the room before I say, "I'd like to wring your little neck." So fast does he sprint back down the stairs and across the basement floor that even going after him as quickly as I can I catch only a flash of his tail as he bolts through the window.

Normally, fixing something around here like a six-by-eight broken window would take perhaps an hour, not including the trip to Swain's for the materials. But this afternoon, for reasons I'm totally aware of, I make a mess of it from the start: taking out what's left of the old glass I cut my thumb twice—not badly, but enough to make it sting and bleed—; I mis-measure the opening for the glass so that I have to go back to Swain's and have them re-cut; and while I'm there the first time I forget the box of points I need. In all, it takes close to three hours to finally replace the window, and when I'm done the idea of "ground beef in the fridge,"—knowing Helen and Teddy are probably eating lobster and filet—doesn't sit too well with me and I decide to bike down to the Ugly Mug for a beer and a club sandwich.

When I come home an hour and a half later, only a tiny

bit of orange left in the sky, I'm startled to see that Teddy's car is back and the downstairs lights, especially those in the small living room to the right, shine warm and yellow through the window. But it's not until I start up the front steps that I hear the music, slow and moody, something that sounds like an arrangement of an old Sinatra song. Instead of going in the front door I walk over to the living room window and look in. The first thing I notice is Teddy's cane lying on the couch. Then I see Helen and Teddy are dancing, not intimately, not even close, but from the expressions on their faces it's certain that this, for them, is a special, even wonderful moment. I watch only for another few seconds and then walk quietly away down the stairs and head up toward Philadelphia Beach. When I come back an hour later Teddy's gone—and Sinatra, too. I go in to see that Helen's reading on the wicker couch, shoes off, a cup of tea to her left. I stand in the doorway looking at her until her eyes come up to mine. Because I say nothing about having seen the two of them, nor will I ever, she is rightfully bewildered when the first thing I say is, "I love you more than I ever have."

THE RIGHT TO SING

It's late Friday afternoon of Easter weekend and instead of being home in Metuchen I'm here in the basement working on an elbow of the 85-year-old cold-water pipe to the kitchen. Helen's in the front hall right above me and has just relayed the news that the phone call was Maureen saying they aren't coming this year because Dennis's partner in the dental practice has had an episode of syncope that's put him in the hospital and left Dennis on call.

When I go upstairs Helen's standing at the open front door, her disappointment clear in how her arms are tightly crossed, her head stern. I stand just behind her for a few moments, my hands black with pipe water and penetrating oil, and look out, too. The light over the ocean is especially pale and two blocks up we hear the waves hit the beach one after another. Helen's long brown hair moves slightly on her shoulders. On the block ours is the only car. Up toward

Madison we see a single figure, a young woman wearing a yellow dress and white sweater. We watch as she looks at each house she passes, then sees our car and starts across the street toward us. Just then Blake and Billie Cranemore turn into the driveway of their ranch across the street. They've replaced last year's red BMW with a light blue one. Billie waves as soon as she gets out and as we go down to meet them I see the young woman change her mind and go back to the other side. On the sidewalk Billie says Blake had a brainstorm at lunch at the Princeton Club and here they are going birding. Over Blake's shoulder I see the young woman slow and look over the BMW. Then Blake asks how our jobs are and when I say fine Billie interrupts the small talk by asking if we're going to rent again this summer to that black family from Connecticut. I stare at her open-mouthed as she turns to Helen and says they rented the last two weeks in June and must have had ten people in the place. Then she says the name, spells it, and asks me to find out from the realtor if they're going to be back. "My understanding," I say, "is that they are African-Americans."

"Whatever," Billie answers.

Helen tells them they have the right to call the police if any tenant is a nuisance. Blake answers it wasn't that bad, just real loud some nights. It seems Billie will never let the matter go, and she presses me again for a promise to see if they've put a deposit on the last two weeks in June. Helen says we'll find out only to bring the conversation to a stop. Blake, sensing the same need to smooth things over, asks us for a drink tomorrow afternoon, and Helen says yes as if all we've been talking about is the weather. On the porch I turn and look back at them going into their house, and then I see the young woman has turned the corner and is now half way up to Beach Avenue.

At five the next afternoon, Blake meets us at the door, drink in hand, and quietly says he's awful sorry for the way Billie acted yesterday but you know how she is, she speaks her mind. As we go in I put a hand on his upper arm and he smiles and asks if gin and tonics are okay. Just as Blake goes into the kitchen Billie comes out, she, too, with a drink. I tell her she's got nothing to worry about in June, the tenants aren't coming back, and she says, "Well, that's good." Then there's a long pause and to fill the awkward space between us she asks if Helen and I are going to church tomorrow. I answer that every Easter we've been here we've gone to the sunrise service at Convention Hall, then headed right home. Billie laughs and says that's way too early for them, that she and Blake'll probably go to the 10:45 at St. Peter's-by-the-Sea, then have lunch at the Lobster House. She asks if I've ever had their Bloody Marys and I answer no. "Just right," she says. Then Billie declares that she and Blake are life-long Episcopalians and point blank asks what we are. I tell her Helen's Presbyterian but that I've never really had a denomination. "But you go with her, don't you?" she asks.

"For the singing," I answer.

"Jack's voice is excellent," Helen says. I blush as she adds that I've got the kind of voice that in church can rise right over everyone else's.

At that moment Blake swears in the kitchen and calls out for Billie. "Oh, what now?" Billie says, her eyes rolling. After a long moment Blake appears in the doorway with one hand out, in the palm a rapidly growing pool of dark blood. Quietly, he explains that in cutting the lime he's run the end of the knife into his hand. He looks down at it as we get to him, and for a few seconds we watch the blood rise in the center. Even though Billie and Helen press paper towels on it, and I hold his wrist as hard as I can, the bleeding is only halved. Blake is remarkably calm, but he's very pale and his mouth is so dry that when he says he'll be all right it's like his tongue's too big.

At the hospital Billie creates so much chaos in the emergency room that a nurse asks Helen to keep her quiet. The three of us sit in soft vinyl chairs in the lounge, Helen in the middle, Billie staring at the frosted glass doors where they've taken Blake. Finally, she gets up and goes straight through them. "You're never going to change a Billie Cranemore," Helen says, then picks up a '*Better Homes and Gardens*' and starts through it.

Right then all hell breaks loose. First there're the sirens outside as three ambulances and two police cars race into the emergency parking area, following them a small yellow school bus and two more police cars. The ambulances contain two older black men on gurneys, both of whom are conscious, and they go right into the same area Blake did. Then almost right away there's a procession of black people who get out of the bus and come through the sliding doors into the waiting room. There are about twenty in all and some of them are hurt, but not very seriously. Their cuts, bruises and whiplashes are consistent with what happened, which I find out from a young man in his late teens who sits down next to me: a semi carrying mail rear-ended them at the last toll booth on the Garden State, not a direct hit, but enough to shoot the bus forward a good fifty yards and hurt the two old men sitting in the back seat. The young man, however, has not been hurt. He is, though, understandably tense for a while until the nurses sort out those in need of immediate care. Then I ask him if he's from around here and he shakes his head and tells me the bus was the choir from Calvary Baptist in Newark on their way to the sunrise service in Cape May. He says he's never been down this way. He's wearing a shiny blue and white basketball jacket and carrying a pocket Bible. I ask if he's in high school and, when he nods, if he plays basketball. "Some," he answers.

"College, then maybe take a shot at the pros?" I ask.

"I want to be a voice teacher," he tells me.

I say I'm Jack Henderson, extend my hand and mention I'm a teacher. He shakes my hand with only his fingers but seems not to hear me. Rather, his eyes go over the room as though all along he's been keeping track of those injured and when they go in and out for care. He watches so closely it's as if they are all his relatives. When he's satisfied everything is all right he sits back in his chair and opens the Bible.

It's then that he puts a hand over his eyes and softly begins to cry. I ask if he's hurt and when he shakes his head, I tell him he's probably in shock, that it hits like that and the best thing to do is just let it out. He slides his hand from his forehead and looks hard at me, his eyes large. "What's with you, mister?" he says and gets up from the chair and goes across the room and out the door. Bewildered, I turn to Helen, who's heard everything and asks what happened. "Nothing," I answer. "Not a thing."

About twenty minutes later as we all go out to the parking lot, Blake's hand bandaged and Billie carrying a prescription, it's dusk. The high yellow lights around the whole area make a ghostly statement against the burned sky. I see the young black man leaning against the side of the school bus, arms folded, the Bible in his right hand, his eyes on me all the way to the car. Even as we drive out, and I glance to the side, he's still looking.

After Billie fills the prescription we decide to go to one of the small restaurants on the outdoor mall downtown, but the first three we come to aren't open for the season yet and we end up in a booth at the Ugly Mug with an NBA game above one end of the bar and a NASCAR race over the other. Blake looks very pale and tired and says his hand already hurts. He says he wants a martini but Billie talks him into light beer and we order a pitcher. Billie buries her head in the menu. I tell her and Blake that if they're looking for something really good they ought to try the chili, that six weeks ago when I was here alone painting I thought it was so good I went back into the kitchen and told the cook it was out of this world. I say he told me it's made by the prep cook at least four days ahead. It surprises me that Billie slaps the menu shut and says that's for her. Blake and Helen order well-done hamburgers.

When the chili turns out to be pretty bad—the kidney beans are crunchy enough that Billie and I can just about hear each other chew—I ask the waitress if the prep cook made it. She tells me the woman was fired a month ago and the cook now does all the chili in the microwave. "My God," the waitress says, "the woman had a temper." I apologize to Billie who shrugs and says it's really not so bad, it's got a good Mexican kick to it.

"More southwestern," I say, to which she answers I could be right, she has a hard time making distinctions like that.

Blake's burger is a small disaster because it's thick enough with tomatoes, onions, pickles and lettuce that it requires both hands to pick it up. Instead, he gets his right hand around it and props the burger up with the left, then tries to take too large a bite and the insides slip out and hang there until he puts it back on his plate. Billie, without a word, reaches over and cuts the burger in quarters. Blake eats just one of them before he winces, looks at his bandaged hand, and says the damn thing's really hurting. When he turns it over I see where blood from the wound has made a small circle right in the middle of the bandages. Billie takes one of the pills from the prescription and gives it to him. While he swallows it with water she picks up his half-full beer glass and empties it into mine. Then she says she thinks we'd better go and I say, after a glance at Helen, that we'll probably walk back along the ocean. Billie says they'll see us in June, and for God's sake no more loud tenants in the house, okay? As the front door swings closed on them I turn to Helen and say, "This chili is absolutely terrible."

Along the boardwalk a nasty southeast wind off the ocean makes things unpleasant and we walk with arms folded and heads down against it until we get to Convention Hall. Inside, lights are on and we see several florist trucks and men carrying in flowers for the service in the morning. Then we hear the piano and quietly I join in with a couple of lines: "Lay hold on life and thou shall see/That Christ is all and all to thee." Helen smiles at me and then we both agree that the wind's got us and turn away to cross Beach Avenue to get away from it.

On our way home nearly all the houses we pass are still shut for the winter, each with some vast emptiness to it that seems unnatural, as though the owners have been dead for generations. As we cross Madison less than a block from our house, and I'm saying I wouldn't miss singing all those great hymns for anything, we both see that sitting boldly on the top step of our stairs is the young woman in the yellow dress from yesterday. When I tell Helen this she says she saw her, too, and thought even then she looked confused. "Maybe she needs help," I say as we approach.

Even though Helen and I stand at the bottom of the

stairs in full view she keeps her gaze above our heads, as though she can see through the houses and motels all the way to the ocean. It's only when Helen asks if we can be of some assistance that she lowers her eyes and looks at us for a long moment. Then she tells us she's looking for work, and before I can ask what kind she says she can do just about anything from yard work to inside painting to cooking, that she's even got a few clients for whom she opens and closes houses for the season, checks them in the winter, does it all. Then she looks away again as if she hears a distant important message. Helen says we're leaving early tomorrow and won't be back until June and we're really not in need of her services. But she is persistent, even edgy, in her request, and Helen says again, this time quite firmly, that there's nothing for her here. The woman suddenly seems to me terribly hurt, even desperate I think, and I move toward her and put a foot on the first stair, my hand on the railing, and ask her what references she might have. She says that last Labor Day weekend she catered the Wilberforce cocktail party next door, did weekly cleaning and cooking for the Kronenberger sisters at the end of the block before they died some years ago, and for the last two years, until she was let go, was the prep cook at the Ugly Mug. When I say, "You make the world's greatest chili," she looks at me and nods and says she sure does. When I ask if she'd give me the recipe she stiffens, says it was her mother's and her grandmother's and no one but her daughter is ever getting it. When I say I'd be willing to buy it from her she says, "I'm just looking for work, sir," and comes down the steps to stand in front of me. "Thanks just the same," she says, and turns to walk off into the darkness.

In the morning as we drive down to Convention Hall the sky is a faint purple and long low clouds hang above the beach, the sort of thin lazy fog that one shot of sunlight will break up. In the darkness the people entering are shadowy and not quite human, but inside the hall where the rows of wooden folding chairs have been set up, the stage arranged with all the flowers, there is warm yellow light everywhere. The curtains along the high windows on the east side are pulled shut, to be opened one after another just as the sun rises over the ocean.

It's not until half way through the second hymn, just as the first curtain is snapped from its window and the light pours over the white-robed singers that I see, as if my eyes are made to go there, that the young black man and the young woman from last night are side by side in the center. Each seems to possess some important human quality I can not in the moment name. Searching, I watch carefully, their faces full of light, and then in the free and powerful way they let go I understand that what they have is humility. It has earned them the right to sing, to exalt.

After the service we start right home, the sun low and bright along the water, and as we leave town and go over the bridge Helen comments on how lovely the service was. Then as we settle onto the Garden State she turns with the question I've been waiting for since the middle of that second hymn. "Why'd you stop so abruptly?" she asks. "Why'd you sit down like that?"

HUMAN D.

Late summer mornings here in Cape May, beginning about six o'clock, are blue and still. Long flat waves climb the beach in white curls, sea birds are motionless on the jetties, and the last of the night air is heavy with water. Along our block the roofs will soon pick up the first rays of sunlight and, for a few minutes, make it dance there. In these moments just before sunrise it seems that much more is possible than it really is.

It is Labor Day weekend and my family and I have come down from Metuchen to close the house. Usually, it's open through the fall when we've gotten away for a few weekends, but this year that free time will be spent visiting colleges with Gary, who has decided he wants to be a vet. Louis, with no interest in the sciences, has shown his poems to Helen, but because I teach at his high school I'll be the last to see them, if ever. Louis is also on the cross-country team, and at this time of year he trains very early in the morning and again in the late afternoon or evening.

On the way downstairs Louis's bed is empty, and I rightly assume I'll find him on the porch after his run. He's in one of the rockers, shoes off, feet up on the railing, hands joined across his middle, looking southeast toward the ocean. His arms and legs are slick with sweat, his breathing slow and very deep. He does not look over as I come out, but a second or two after the screen door closes he quietly says, "Hi." I say good morning and ask if he wants anything from the kitchen, that I'm going for some cereal and coffee. He startles me by saying that in a couple of years I'll be looking at 50. He adds, "Do you think about dying?"

"Sometimes," I say.

"What do you think it's like?" he asks.

Ordinarily, I am not uncomfortable with Louis's questions, but right now there is a persistent, nerveless tone in his voice I've not heard before. "Depends," I say, avoiding him. Then I add, "I don't think my father knew what hit him."

"Suppose he did," Louis says.

I sit down on the railing by the porch column so that I have a better look at him, then cross my arms and say, "That's possible." His body is a runner's—thin, long, and in the calves and thighs very strong. In the early morning humidity the sweat will not go away. "What is it?" I say directly, then unfold my arms and put my hands on the railing.

In a steady, flat voice he tells me that last Monday at practice he found out that his first girlfriend, someone he hasn't seen in two years because she goes to the Catholic high school now, has leukemia. For a second he struggles with the word, *virulent*. His face flashes anger, especially around the mouth, his eyes lost and dark. He looks back to the ocean, then tells me that for the last month she's been at Sloan-Kettering in New York. Then he asks quietly, "Is she bald?"

"I don't know," I say.

He tells me he wrote her a letter, that he thought about it for several days and then did it, sent it directly to her at the hospital. I ask him how he got the address and he says at the library. Then he gets up, goes down the front steps and around to the back of the house to the outside shower under the kitchen window.

As I put an English muffin in the toaster and get down the cereal boxes and bowls I hear the water start and look out. I think of several things I might tell him, then realize they would be worthless, and that, finally, I can do nothing. I watch the water fall straight down on his head, as if he were a boy.

Helen, dressed in shorts and one of my old shirts tied at the middle, comes into the kitchen. She is still sleepy, but right away she knows something's wrong. She stops, a hand on the sink, and I tell her. She knew the girl better than I, the mother vaguely, and she takes the news like someone's smacked her. There is a moment when the only sound is the light banging of the water pipes in the basement as Louis shuts off the faucets, then our eyes meet. "What is she, sixteen?" Helen says.

In the afternoon Louis asks if I'll drive him out to the Point so he can get the mileage exact for his run the next morning, that he wants it to be right on eight miles. His voice is lost, as though the girl is nearby and he's saying it to her. As we drive out Lafayette there are heavy clouds far out over the bay and I know we'll have rain by the evening.

The parking lot between the shell shop and the hot dog stand is packed with holiday cars and families coming and going from the beach. It is unlike the last time we were here, on a gray and chilly June evening, the four of us eating chicken and cole slaw from the Filling Station, time stopped, the boys and I passing a beer behind Helen's back, laughter from one or the other of us for no discernible reason.

Just as I start the car to leave a large sea gull flies toward us over the low inland trees, wobbling horribly, and crashes into the back of one of the wooden benches, flips over it, and comes to rest, belly up, on the seat, a wing jammed between the slats. Louis, as though he thinks he can help the bird, hurries out of the car and runs the few yards to it. Then he stops and looks down. When I come up behind him I see that on the smooth curve of its chest is a small bullet hole, the contrast of the blood with the stark white feathers so vivid it seems painted there.

When I say who the hell would do such a thing he answers, "Some kid." Louis reaches out to try to free the wing and then, in a way that will return to me at unexpected times—in class, falling asleep, at a red light—the gull in one last reflex smacks its beak hard into the center of Louis's palm, briefly pinning it hard to the wood. He jerks away, more amazed than hurt, and looks at it. The skin is not broken but almost immediately a red circle begins to form, under it a small dark place where the blood vessels have broken.

Then the gull, all on its own, slides off the bench and falls heavily onto the sandy blacktop, its head at an impossible angle, wings extended. I watch Louis opening and closing his hand and ask if he's okay. When he nods I say, "Senseless," my eyes going back and forth between the gull and him. Then there is a moment in which we both look at the gull, now not more than an awkward collection of angles, and then as I turn away Louis says, "Are you just going to leave it there?"

"What should I do?" I ask.

As we drive back toward town the sharp light of the afternoon has dimmed from the clouds behind us. For a short while it is the kind of rare light from an eclipse. "What'd you write her?" I ask. He says it was cross-country, about coming down here for the weekend, his fears of calculus, and ends with the statement, looking out the side window, that it wasn't anything special. As we drive the lighthouse, tall and grand in the distance, moves above the trees.

"What was your father like?" Louis asks. His voice is direct, his eyes out to the right on the lighthouse and the great swirls of birds moving in endless circles above it.

"Most of the time," I say, "he was all right." Then I add, "When he wasn't drinking."

"He beat you, didn't he?" Louis says. I turn and look at him, then ask in an even voice how he knows that. He says, more flat than I am, that his grandmother, Verna, told him last year. "He mess with Uncle Phil?" he asks. I tell him just once and that Phil, who is older, stood his ground, said if he hit him he'd call the police. Then I smile, remembering the day I lifted the phone and pointed at my father and said, "I *will.*" I tell Louis this and when he asks what happened I say that my father never touched me again.

"A transfer of power," Louis says.

"Where'd you get that?" I ask, still with the same smile.

"'Human D.,'" he says, the reference to one of his electives last year. When I turn to look at him I see the skin along his jaw line is so fine it's almost transparent, under it a few tiny veins like my father had.

In the early evening, Helen and I on the porch, the ocean full of pinks and curious greens from the sunset, Louis sits on the top of the stairs, his back against one of the columns, legs straight out, looking toward the ocean. Now and again he glances at us for a long moment as though our presence is something remarkable to him, then looks back to the street and ocean. I have never seen him so still. After a few moments he gets up as if we are not there and goes into the house. Helen, her voice more empty than I have ever heard it, asks about the bruise on Louis's palm and I tell her briefly about the gull. She looks away and after a long, thoughtful moment says, "What can I say to him?"

Louis comes out the door dressed only in running shorts and anklet socks, his shoes dangling from one hand. Wordlessly, in the growing dusk, he sits on the top step and puts the shoes on, ties them in double bows, and then quickly goes down the stairs, veering to the left as he does, ducks under the branches of a new, small maple the city planted in June, and begins to run. As he crosses Philadelphia, only 50 or 60 yards away, we both lose sight of him.

Helen and I have some feeble conversation about when the house might need painting again, and then she remembers that the mother is single, the girl her only child. A light breeze moves through the long porch. It has a warm, lilac fragrance. Coming from the same direction Louis went in two joggers, a man and woman, laugh in a choppy, breathless way. Round and happy, they go by in identical gray sweat shirts and white running shorts.   Then   we   are quiet for what seems a long time, the silence broken finally by the sound of light rain that first softly strikes the porch roof and then the stiff leaves on the trees close by. "I wonder how you go on after something like that," Helen says. I answer softly that I don't know, that everything must be changed. "Probably part of you doesn't," Helen says, as if to herself.

In a few minutes it is raining hard enough that the air has an abnormal chill, the warmth from the day gone in a flash, a damp October feeling everywhere. Exactly at the same time we look at each other. Lightly, she says she wonders if Louis is all right in the rain and I answer that for runners rain is air conditioning. Her face does not register that I have spoken. Rather, there is a darkness to it as she fixes her eyes in the direction Louis went. Neither of us speaks for several long moments and then, finally, Helen asks how long he's been gone. "Usual," I say, "about a half hour." When she says she thinks it's longer I shake my head and tell her no, it's not quite that. I know that it's actually been almost 40 minutes since he left and that considering his evening run is usually the shorter of the two I know he's ten to 15 minutes overdue.

Then walking toward us through the rain come Blake and Billie Cranemore, their Yorkie on a leash between them, she carrying her scotch in a Ronald McDonald glass, he his beer in an oversized plastic cup with *Go Giants!* on the side. They wear identical L.L. Bean slickers, Billie barefoot, Blake in laceless old tennis shoes. Helen, with her mouth slightly open, and without moving her lips, manages to say clearly, but very softly, "Oh, no." Once a summer, either in June or now, they surprise us with an evening visit, appearing with at least a half-hour's supply of alcohol, a mental list of grievances concerning the summer's tenants, and political views from the French and Indian War. Everything in their lives, so far as we know, concerns money.

As soon as they sit down, Helen turns her head slightly away from Billie to look out over the porch railing into the darkness. I feel her anxiety about Louis, and when she looks back I try to catch her eye, but she's absorbed by Blake saying that he heard the old Kronenberger sisters' house had been sold again, this time to a doctor from Philadelphia. "Originally from New Delhi," he adds and rolls his eyes at Billie who, with a sip of scotch in her mouth, giggles. Then I feel the same pull that Helen did, and I turn in my chair to look past Blake. Nothing moves at all in the darkness on our street, and just for an instant I feel that Louis has disappeared for good. When I look back at Helen her eyes are wide and black in the dim light.

As Blake berates the President as too cautious and too political, Billie nodding, lips puffy and shiny, the phone rings. Gary answers it almost right away and then calls out to ask if Louis is on the porch with us. Helen tells him, in a slightly raised voice, that he's running. "In this?" Gary says, and Helen tells him to take a message. Then after he hangs up Helen calls to ask who was on the phone. "Some girl," Gary answers.

The next 20 minutes go by slowly, our concentration more and more shallow, Helen half the time with her head turned toward the street, nodding to be polite. Finally, it is Blake who says he thinks he and Billie ought to be getting along, that Lance will soon need his evening trot. Helen and I both stare at him, then Helen says she thought the dog's name was Rex and Billie tells us that Rex died over the winter and they bought Lance last December. "Seen one Yorkie...," Blake says as he rises and extends a hand to

Billie. He pulls her straight up out of the chair. Briefly, both are slightly unsteady, then just fine. It is as they go down the stairs, each with a hand on the railing, that Louis appears walking slowly out of the rain and darkness. He is shiny with water, his hair flat, his running shorts glued to his middle. The Cranemores regard him as though he's an apparition, then Billie says in a startled way, "Oh, hello, Louie," then takes Blake's arm, and together they step off the curb.

Louis stands at the bottom of the steps looking up at us, hands on his hips, as though he wants to stay in the rain. "That was a long run," I say.

"I went out to the Point," he answers. When neither of us says anything he adds, "To bury the gull." He looks from Helen to me, keeps his eyes hard on mine, then says, "But there wasn't much left of it." It's when he starts up the stairs that Helen and I see that both his knees have been badly skinned, and that the blood has mixed with the rain to make his shins and ankles pink. He anticipates our concern and says he fell going over a curb in town on the way out, then shows us his hands and where the heels are the same as his knees. Small bits of gravel look to be imbedded in the skin.

Inside, draped over the phone by Gary, is a yellow legal sheet on which was a small portion of a draft of a college application essay, now abandoned. On the top of the paper is a telephone number, the area code for New York City, underneath it, "Old Jill?" As if we aren't there, Louis looks at it for a long moment and then sets it down. He goes straight up the stairs to shower and, as he did once before when he fell, to scrub the dirt and tiny pebbles from the wounds.

Helen asks if I want a glass of tea and I shake my head and go back out to the porch and sit down. The rain is slow now and moves through the white cones from the street lights over on Philadelphia in lazy mists. Now and then a car hisses along the street, the water silver under its wheels, its lights blunt. I think of my father dying at 47, sitting under a tree in the deep Pennsylvania woods, his rifle across his lap, in the picture a family of deer curious and serene in their inspection of him. Right then Helen comes out with her tea. She is quiet for a long time. "What would you say to her?" she asks.

"I don't have to talk to her," I answer. Then, after a moment, I add, "Christ, I don't know."

When she says, looking straight into the night, that it isn't fair, I nod. And when she says a lot of kids get well I answer, "Some." Then behind us the door to the house closes softly, its latch like a finger snap, and we both know that Louis is calling. After a long silence we hear Louis's muffled voice through the half-open windows to either side of us, and then he laughs. Helen and I look at each other as if to verify what we've heard, then we are bewildered as he laughs again, the sound natural and full of pleasure. "For God's sake," Helen says softly, and I add, "What's he doing?" in a tone as quiet as hers. Then Louis yells up the stairs to Gary, his voice light and ironic. "Gar?" he says, "why do the sisters at St. Joe's travel in pairs?" Before Gary can answer Louis calls, "One reads, the other writes." After a moment Gary answers, "God is listening," and we hear his door slam. Louis is quiet then on the phone, and just as I make the assumption that his talk with the girl is now more serious, even formal, he laughs again, clearly says, "Come on," and follows it with something that sounds like, "No way." Then there is a long exchange between them which Helen and I hear only in modulating snatches: his cross-country and her chemotherapy receive equal time, as though they are somehow normal extra-curricular activities.

He asks more about what a white-cell count means, and then he uses the words, "Bone marrow." After a moment he says, innocently, "They can do that?", then a long pause followed by, "Amazing."

A burst of rain on the porch roof smothers Louis's voice, the sound like drumming finger nails or baby hooves, and I am relieved not to hear him. For a while we are quiet, then Helen says she wonders if the girl's really got a chance, and just as I turn to her the single bare bulb of the overhead porch light snaps on, a watery white everywhere, and Louis comes out. He looks angry and confused. On his knees are the two half-dollar-size scrapes, each shiny and oozing. They will cause him plenty of pain both in the night and when he runs again. "How're your hands?" I ask, and he turns them over, fingers bent, to show us. The heels are purple, as though they have been struck again and again with a hammer, and in the shadows they look black and nearly crippled.

Right then Gary calls down that he wants one of us to come and read his essay. Helen glances at Louis, then me, and says she'll go. As she passes Louis she puts a hand on his shoulder, which he seems not to notice, then goes inside where, after a few seconds, she turns out the light. The darkness makes the rain louder and more insistent. As Louis sits in Helen's chair he flinches from bending his knees, then covers it quickly. Finally, he glances away toward the street, his eyes steady as though he can see the rain. He says, "She told me God's on her side and everything's going to be all right." He turns to me. "You believe in God?" he asks, a clear challenge in his voice.

"Sometimes," I answer

"Yes or no," he says.

"Then yes."

"That's pretty weak."

"It's the best I can do," I tell him.

In bending his knees he has opened the scrapes and two small lines of watery blood are an inch or so down his shins. His face, even in the poor light, seems transformed, the bones harder and more mature, his cheeks concave, the jaw line a pale marble. I ask him then if the girl will have a bone-marrow transplant and he nods and says if they can find a donor, that for the last month and a half something about her blood type has been the problem. He adds that they are even looking for her father. His face tenses as if from a passing anger, then the small muscles go flat and hold everything in. "No one can prove there's a God," he says quietly.

"Nor that there isn't," I answer.

"I know, I know," he says, a hand rising slightly in a small, defiant gesture. Then he is still, his body almost rigid, and he makes the statement, "There isn't anything to say, is there?" He turns so that our eyes meet, and through the darkness the distance between us seems huge. In answer, I shake my head slowly and he looks away. Then his face suddenly shatters into hard, sad angles, a powerful surge of feeling taking over. I want to reach out to him, take him into my arms as if he's still a child and I could be all that he needs. But I do nothing because this is his moment and I know he must do the suffering of it by himself, that the only thing I have to give him is silence.

After a few moments he is very calm and comes forward a little in the chair. He slides his fingers through a long line of thick water pooled along the flat surface of the porch railing. He taps it a couple of times and it makes a tiny splash. Then he opens his hand fully, turns it over, and rests it on the flat surface to allow a small puddle to form there.

He brings the water to his mouth, presses his lips into the skin to take in what he can. As he turns to look at me he smiles slightly, then puts his hand back on the railing to collect more water. I see, just barely, the dark spot in the middle of his palm, and then I put my hand out, a ways away from his, to feel the cool rain. I know, of course, that in all the time ahead the beak of that gull will come down again and again, sometimes to go straight through to the wood, but even that, in this moment, is all right, too.

MIDDLE AGE

Here on Philadelphia Beach my mother, Verna, sits in an aluminum folding chair down by the water, legs crossed like a man, the back of her floral one-piece suit a *U*, head tilted for the sun as if at 72 her only worry is the imminent death of her old cat, George, who at this moment sleeps in the middle of her bed back at the house. Before she picked up her chair about half an hour ago and went down to the water, we had a long conversation about my being acting head of the English department, and how Helen's finally gotten full-time library work now that Gary's in college and Louis will be next year. She listened, nodding from time to time, I a little full of myself with a one-year administrative role that, I admitted to her, I liked and might pursue on a permanent basis. After a pause she said I ought to do what I wanted and when because age is a funny thing, one day you've just got a bad case of it. Her eyes darted from the ocean to the jetty, then back to her hands in her lap. "George isn't going to live much longer," she said from nowhere. When I asked what the vet had said she answered, "Bumps along his back." Then after a few moments of silence she stood and put her hand on the back of the chair and lifted it out of the sand. It took a lot more effort than she thought.

Helen arrives in her suit carrying a small red and white cooler. Her expression says I'd better keep quiet for a few minutes. She kneels, sits back on the soles of her feet, opens the cooler, and takes out two small yogurts. When I shake my head she drops one back inside. Her eyes on Verna, she asks how she is. When I nod she says, "Gary's Christian business has got to go." She looks as though she's had a short cry during the two-block walk down here. Then she adds it's all because he met Miss Chastity Self-righteousness at the campus ministry and can't figure out a way to get into her pants. Still looking at Verna, and still holding the yogurt, she says she asked him just who he thought was going to pay for his year off serving the Lord in Appalachia with Miss What's-Her-Face Missionary. She catches me as I roll my eyes slightly. "Oh, yes," she says. "Oh, yes." I ask if she thinks we ought to flatly say no, he has to go on now with his pre-vet major, and see what happens. She answers why not, since we're already Philistines anyway.

Later, as we go up the front steps to our porch, Verna between us, our sons give us news, Gary first with the time Mary's coming from Wildwood for dinner—five sharp—then Louis with a report that George is making hideous sounds. Instead of the stooped frail woman between Helen and me there's someone now tense and very alert. A hand on the banister, she goes up the stairs as quickly as she can. Helen and I follow, I close behind in case she misses a step. At the top we hear George in her bedroom at the front of the house, his sounds just as Louis described. In the room George is stretched out on the bed so that he seems nearly twice as long. His chest heaves with each throaty noise, his eyes, even from where Helen and I stand by the door, as though he's already dead. Verna kneels by the side of the low bed, both arms out to George. In this awkward position I see the bones of her unbearably thin pelvis, as though they have been made from the finest wood. She strokes his head with one hand, the other gentle and quiet on his rear legs, and softly says his name, then something else with *mommy* buried in it.

When the phone rings downstairs Gary calls up that it's for Helen. She puts a hand on my arm and leaves silently, half closing the door on her way. I go around to the other side of the bed and sit near the foot. I don't think Verna even knows I'm still there until she looks up for a second and stares at me like I'm a stranger. She seems completely unprepared for George's dying, as though until just a few minutes ago his illness had been theory. Now, though, her eyes are watery and wide with astonishment that, in fact, in a little while George will be dead. Her hand moves along his side so lightly that George's hair actually rises to meet it. His sounds are steady and between his teeth there is a dot of pale tongue. Between breaths, which are slowing slightly, his heart is wild against his ribs. She asks if I think he's suffering and when I look again at his eyes, the pupils now tiny black buttons, I say no, he's in coma. She moves back a bit then, her eyes still on him, and rises with some difficulty. I ask what I can do and she shakes her head, tears running straight down her cheeks, and says he's her baby and she doesn't know what she'll do without him.

I go into our bedroom just as Helen comes down the hall. When I ask who phoned she says it was the great news that we're pre-approved for a Visa card from the Bank of Guam. As soon as the door's closed she asks how long I think George has. I tell her it's impossible to say but that Gary might know, and her eyes widen a little and she says he could probably get the answer directly from the Lord. She catches herself right away and says she's sorry, but wouldn't you know George'd do it now, right when her mother's on her way.

She has a point. Our mothers have not seen each other since our wedding nearly 23 years ago. The few times Verna's visited Mary's been away from Wildwood either seeing her sister in Tempe or Maureen. Over the years they've had one exchange of letters. Mel died shortly after he and Mary had been divorced, and Verna wrote Mary that she should realize that for her Mel died twice. Although Mary never showed us the letter she mentioned what it meant to her for years afterwards and has always asked how Verna was getting along. Right now, if she could hear the sobbing from across the hall, she'd know not too well. When Helen says that, for God's sake, it's only a cat we look at each other for a long moment and for the second time since she's closed the door she says she's sorry.

Right at the moment Helen takes off her suit we hear two light taps on Mary's car horn. Helen holds the suit close to her and leans her head out the window to call to Mary to come in, we'll be right down. "I don't know what to do for her," I say to Helen, who turns to look at me.

On the porch, Verna and Mary sit next to each other on the other side of the small white wicker table, Helen across from them, Louis and Gary off to the side on the railing. Helen places the coasters next to the napkins that have small piles of nuts and tiny pretzels on them, and I set the drinks down. Mary, older but in better health and with a quickness to her that left Verna about a year ago, has heard about a Mexican earthquake on the car radio and she's full of approximate numbers of the dead and missing, as well as damage estimates and the potential for aftershocks. Verna is affected by this and sits looking at Mary as though she'd been there. When Mary concludes that, "California's due again, too," Verna nods.

As Mary sips the gin and tonic Helen tells her about George, all the while Mary looking at Verna. There is clearly a connection I see them suddenly make, an instant in which they know they like each other. Gary and Louis, bored with the four of us, leave with polite excuses, then Mary and Verna begin a conversation that excludes Helen and me. This makes me uncomfortable and a little irritated, but when I look at Helen she is remarkably serene. Twice I offer comments I hope will allow me into the conversation, which go unanswered, and it's only after a glance at Helen, who gives me a quizzical look, that I take a handful of pretzels, sit back, and shut up.

Within a few minutes Gary comes through the screen door, shuts it quietly, then walks over to Helen, leans down, and whispers in her ear. Verna and Mary take no notice of him, but I know from the look on Helen's face that George is dead. Then as if Verna and Mary sense it, too, they turn to Helen and Gary. Verna looks like she's going to say something but then turns her head toward the street. Mary puts a hand on Verna's along the arm of the chair and lets it rest there. "You're sure?" Helen says to Gary, who's a little indignant that his clinical observation has been challenged. He answers that George is already getting cold but that rigor has not yet begun. "What do we do?" Verna asks, the question so general it floats among us all. Gary, anxious to impress, says there's a window of several hours in which to decide, but after that, if George isn't frozen, decomposition will onset. I want to correct his word usage but catch myself and look back to Verna. Her eyes have filled with huge tears, but she is otherwise in control of herself, and I see that Mary has tightened her grip on her hand. Then when Verna says she wants to take George home I make the mistake of asking what she'll do with him there. Mary answers for her. "Whatever she wants," she says and pats Verna's hand. Gary, quicker than Helen or I, says he'll get George ready for the freezer.

With the logistics of George's preservation clear Verna now allows herself a moment of grief. With Mary still holding one hand Verna covers her eyes with the other and cries in a hard, silent way. Louis tries to supply some comfort and says to Verna that she can always get another cat, right? Mary answers again for Verna, who, with eyes still down, gives no indication that she's heard Louis. "No," Mary says to him gently, "that wouldn't be fair to the cat." It takes Louis a moment to understand and then his face goes flat and he stares at Verna as though for the first time he knows his grandmother will not live forever. In this moment I don't know whom to help, and so I choose George, get up, and go inside to the bottom of the stairs just as Gary's bringing him down wrapped in a small yellow blanket. In the kitchen Gary holds George and looks at me as though I work for him and he's already given me the order to clear out the freezer. Easier said than done, I realize. George is no package of lima beans, and the old refrigerator's freezer compartment has to be at least half empty to fit him in. I tell Gary to go ask his mother what she wants to do with the frozen foods and, George in front of him, he starts down the hall. "No, no," I tell him, "put the cat down." He sets George on the edge of the sink, then turns away and hurries back down the hall. Slowly, part of the blanket slides off George so that only the first fold is over his middle. It's then I notice he seems to be looking at me, his final expression one that says death is all right if you belong to someone.

Helen comes in, Gary right behind her, and walks over to the freezer as if I'm not there. One glance at George and one at the frozen food and she says this changes dinner, all right, and takes out two packages of peas and the London broil, a big bag of French fries and the dozen under-ten shrimp from the Lobster House we were saving for our last night here. The food out, George, rewrapped, goes in. As Helen puts the meat in the microwave and punches up the defrost settings, she says I could make everyone another drink, and I answer that I'm sorry Verna wants to take George home but it's not for me to tell her no. "The cat," she says as she pokes the start button on the microwave, "is going to be in there for a week."

At dinner, which is only about a half hour later than planned, it is clear that while Helen and I have taken care of George and the food preparation, Verna and Mary have bonded so thoroughly that when I suggest seating arrangements at the table, each mother next to her child, Mary takes Verna's hand and says, pointing, that they're both sitting on the window side because the early evening sun will feel good. That leaves Helen and me across from them, the boys at either end.

As soon as we start Helen realizes she's forgotten the

peas in the microwave and goes back to the kitchen. Gary picks that moment, when I have a mouthful of steak, to say he's decided to go back to Rutgers and not take the year off. Verna, in two simple compound sentences, explains to Mary. I watch Louis take a handful of French fries directly from the bowl and put them on his plate. When he sees I've observed this he makes no apology. Rather, he points at the ketchup, then gives me a patronizing smile as though I'm a minor enemy just vanquished. Slowly, I turn to ask Gary what has brought on this sudden reversal and he looks from Verna and Mary to me and says, "Hey, my life, right?"

"So it is," I answer. But it's not enough. I want to know the motivation and prod the issue. "But you were so definite," I say to Gary.

"That was then, this is now," he answers.

"Guy decided not to go," Louis puts in. I give him a glance that says he doesn't belong in this conversation, but it has no effect. Just as I turn back to Gary ready to ask when he'll inform the girl and how he thinks she'll take the news, Helen comes in carrying the steaming peas in a large white serving dish. "Hot," she says, "very hot," and sets the bowl in the middle of the table. Instantly, Louis gives her the news. Her reaction surprises me. "How nice," she says, turning to Gary, and then as she walks past my chair she lets a hand go over my shoulders. Gary says he just decided it wasn't for him. "Better sooner than later," Helen says, smiling, as she sits down.

I pick up the peas and offer them to Louis. He looks at me as though he's never seen me before, then takes the bowl and passes it to Mary. When I stare at him for a moment he says, "Want me to throw up?"

"*Louis*," Helen says, then explains quickly to Verna and Mary his childhood history with peas.

"Why'd he tease me with the bowl?" Louis asks.

"One day you'll like peas," I tell Louis.

"I think not," he answers slowly.

"He just wants to control everything," Gary says.

After dinner when the last of the light is no more than a dark red mist and the air is so still that the sound of the waves gets the two blocks back to where we're on the porch with coffee, Verna seems uncomfortable, even a little agitated. Her thumbs scrape across her finger tips in a steady, futile rhythm, and from the way she turns her head it's as though she's waiting for someone she loves who's long overdue. As though it is a condition she understands, Mary makes conversation with her in a careful, affectionate way, Helen and I included as though to signal us how Verna's feeling. In all that Mary says about how the weather's been this season, how the blues are running, and the progress of the dredging in Wildwood, Verna only now and again glances at her, then looks at Helen and me in a quick, nervous way, as though she has something important to give us and doesn't know how to do it. In the fading light it seems her body grows smaller, her bare arms almost translucent. Only in her eyes is there a powerful clearness, as though throughout the day she has stored a small degree of light that now wants out.

Within a few minutes Mary says she and Verna are going for a walk, perhaps down to the beach, perhaps to the boardwalk, and right away I object saying that within the hour, maybe even minutes, the fog will come in as it has every night all week, that it'll be damp and there'll be a chill. Neither seems to hear me and when Helen rests a hand on my arm I have no trouble with its signal. Verna gets her light blue windbreaker from the hat rack inside the front door, and, down on the sidewalk, Mary stops at the car for a sweater, then they go together, slowly, along New York Avenue toward the center of town.   It's then that we hear sharp words from upstairs between Gary and Louis, and although we can not make out exactly what the squabble's about there's no mistaking the swear words each uses. I go open the screen door and put my head inside to tell them to please hold it down, after all we've got neighbors. This is met with silence followed by suppressed laughter as, no doubt, one has said something to the other about me.

Helen and I talk for a while about how Verna and Mary have hit it off so well, and then Gary and Louis come down and ask for the car keys, say they're going down to the boardwalk for a while and hang out, maybe even drive out to the Point. When I'm slow to hand them over Helen tells Gary to take her set on the counter by the back door. We don't say anything until they drive off, perhaps a little too fast through the fog, and for several minutes after they're gone Helen stays quiet. Then I ask if she thinks I ought to get out of administration and she nods slowly and emphatically, as if she's been waiting for the question a long time. I tell her I think it's probably a good idea and ask if she thinks I've changed over the last year. "Not a lot," she says.

Then we get our jackets from inside and start down toward the beach through the fog. From the house it looked to be dense, but as we walk it's not that at all. There's a strange pattern to it, first a thick patch, then nothing, then it's back again. Just as we get to Beach Avenue, the sound of the waves subdued by the fog, I catch a glimpse of Verna and Mary standing side by side down the way on the end of the boardwalk, the dim green and red neon from the motels making them seem like dashboard statues. Helen sees them, too, and stops. When I say let's go see how they're doing Helen makes no response. Rather, she steps back a little, reluctant to cross the street, hands in her jacket pockets. What little traffic there is moves slowly behind headlights able to do little in the fog. When I see a chance to cross the street I touch her arm and am surprised that it's rigid, as if her body has gone stiff with purpose. "Let's go," I say after another glance at the traffic.

"No," she says. She looks at them with clear bright eyes.

"What is it?" I ask.

"You don't see what I see," she answers. I look back toward Verna and Mary, who stand so close their arms could be linked. For the first time I realize they are nearly the same height. "Us," Helen says, "then the boys, then their kids, all going along."

It takes a moment but I finally understand. "There's a line from Whitman," I say.

"I'm sure there is," she answers, her eyes still hard on Verna and Mary.

I let it go and look back at Verna and Mary just as an especially dense cloud rolls in over the beach and consumes them. Right then, as if intentionally meant to break the moment, our car comes along Beach Avenue through the fog, Gary at the wheel, Louis with his window rolled down, an elbow out. Astonishingly, he's smoking a cigar, which he discards directly toward the curb where Helen and I are standing. It tumbles along the wet pavement in a lovely spiral of sparks and then is crushed by the front tire of a Chevy pickup. We watch them go down toward Convention Hall, and then I say to Helen that they didn't see us. She answers she's grateful for small things, then asks if I'm going to say something to Louis about smoking. Just as I'm about to say of course I will I look back to see that Verna and Mary are gone, that in the fog they have slipped away without a trace. After a moment, I ask Helen if she thinks Gary was right at dinner when he said I want to control everything.

"What you want," she says, "is to have your family back."

DEBTS

It's nine-thirty on a showery Friday night in early June and Helen and I are sitting in Louis's seven-year-old Hyundai in front of the house. We ought to be delighted with the evening—we've just come from the rehearsal dinner at the Peter Shield's Inn for Gary's wedding tomorrow afternoon—but we're exhausted. Helen found out two days ago that she has to have a lumpectomy, "a.s.a.p.," as Dr. Theodora put it, but right away she made up her mind she wasn't ruining these two days for anything. She's been tight as a drum since yesterday morning when we drove down from Metuchen, her attitude that of someone with no more on her mind than a wisdom-tooth problem. On the dark red hood of the car tiny marbles of water hold starlight. Helen, her face resolute, stares ahead. The Hamptons, she says of Sally's parents, are lovely people. She says we're all going to get along so well. Then she moves a hand to the side of her left breast and shifts uneasily. In answer to my question if she still has pain from the biopsy she nods and says some under the arm, but mostly it's in her head. A very light rain touches the windshield and in the streetlight down the block thin patches of fog drift by. When she asks how she was this evening—she says she couldn't stop her hand shaking when she gave her toast—I tell her she got through with flying colors. Then we're silent for a long moment. When I say Louis made a very funny toast she smiles and says he did, but her voice is melancholy and distant. Then out of the blue she asks if she died would I remarry. "Come on," I say, but she presses the question and after a moment I tell her I would right away, probably that afternoon. She calls me a wise-ass and looks out the window. "Truth is," I say, "I don't know what I'd do without you." She asks if she's been a good mother and when I tell her of course she says and good for you? Why the inventory I ask and she says they're just questions she has at night.

Right then Louis drives up in our station wagon with Gary and the four ushers, two from vet school, two old friends from Rutgers, and parks in front of us. In their lights they've seen we're still in the car, and Louis and Gary come over while the others hurry into the house, some already carrying their jackets and ties. I put my window down and Louis leans over and says he's Inspector Callahan and I'd better not try anything funny with the little lady. Then Gary behind him senses something's not right and asks what's up. Helen smiles and says she's just never had a son get married before, then Louis interrupts with the news that he and Gary and Sally have decided to run the Great Cape May Foot Race, a 10K scheduled for eight-thirty in the morning. He adds it's no problem since the wedding's not 'till four. Then Gary says everybody's going swimming now and after that back to the Peter Shield's bar. He pushes off from the car and puts his arm around Gary and together they go up the steps into the house. "Some things I can not imagine," Helen says. As she watches them her face empties in a hard, quick way, as though some tiny portion of her soul is visible for a second. Then she stares again into the darkness like she's able to make out something or someone. So intently does she look, tears in her eyes instantly, that I turn my head, too, but nothing's there. I think that finally she's going to let her feelings out and I put my arm around her. But she doesn't. She only leans into me, her body light and soft, like the bones have lost half their weight.

As soon as we go inside, Helen's all business. For luncheon tomorrow—Maureen's family is coming from Red Bank and my brother's gang from New Haven—she's made a seven-layer chocolate cake we transported yesterday so carefully packed it looked like a bomb, and all that now remains is the final coat of icing. In the kitchen we are nearly wordless as she works, and she seems as lost in the effort as a sculptor. Only twice do I bring up the subject, once to say I think the boys should know and the second that at least she should tell Maureen tomorrow. Her first answer is an emphatic not now, the second that her sister, although a love, is first cousin to Chicken Little. "No, thanks," she says, stepping back from the cake, her eyes all over it. She cocks her head and says she hopes it's enough for everyone. Then with great care she wets a dish towel and lovingly wipes clean the edges of the spode plate. Finally, she places the glass cover over it and asks me to carry it into the dining room where I put it directly in the center of the table. It looks like it's come from the best bakery in the world.

Upstairs, Helen's asleep almost as soon as she lies down, her face so relaxed the muscles seem to have melted a little.

Her mouth is slightly open, her breathing deep and regular. I turn off the lamp on the small table by her side of the bed as quietly as I can. In the fresh darkness I feel her presence, her breathing what I've heard next to me for all these years, and I can not imagine being alone. As I walk to the window the wide floor boards make familiar sounds. The wind and water combine in tight, wiggling streaks on the panes, and long capes of light rain slide along the street. I will not permit words because language will soften my feelings, make their edges smooth and round. Words like *love*, *years*, *time*, *fear*, *grief* rise singly, each seeking its proper place in a sentence meant to organize and console, as though I should coax myself into an understanding or, better still, a working-through. Tell that to the fish out there, I think.

Then comes a stillness nearly unbearable, as though time has truly stopped, the feeling like quarry-jumping at night. A gust of wind shakes and bends the screen and more water hits the panes. I think of Gary, a vet now for three years, and Sally, in her first year as a public defender, and wonder what their life together will be like. I remember us starting out and how it feels like only a week or two ago. A car's headlights come through the steady drizzle straight down the middle of the street. Helen stirs and makes a small sound with her mouth and lips followed by a light moan, as though only in sleep can she allow a true feeling. I turn to look at her on her side, her legs now straight out. In the cool light of the room it looks like she's in a black-and-white movie, as though she's been scooped up by time and hurled ahead to a place I can't get to. She is, I think finally, just helpless, and so am I. I go to my side of the bed and get in quietly and stretch out, then put my hand on the edge of her pillow so I can feel her breath on my wrist.

I'm on the porch just after seven when Gary comes out carrying a bowl of Cheerios and a banana. What he'd really like, he says, is a piece of that chocolate cake. Before I can answer he says, "I know, touch it and die." Then he nods toward the street and says the humidity during the race is going to be murder. Just as he raises a spoonful of the cereal he straightens a forefinger and says late last night your old friend, Horse, called to say he was driving down this morning from Philly. When I say oh, no, and ask why Gary says to run the race.

Horse got his nickname from the students in the high school where we both taught for his large awkward jaw and a laugh you could hear two classrooms away. The four times I've seen him, ever since I came to his defense at the administrative hearing last year where he was fired for alcoholism (he did get a year's salary out of them to get back on his feet) he wags a finger at me and says he owes me, that if there's anything he can ever do for me or Helen all I've got to do is say the word. He's been dry now for over a year and acts like Helen and I are dear relatives, which means he feels he can show up unexpectedly and do things like put his feet on the coffee table and help himself to whatever he finds in the refrigerator. But there's something about him truly likeable, a warm charm, a child's directness, as though he still sees everything with a clear, innocent eye. It's what made him such a splendid teacher.

I'm just about to say to Gary that his mother's going to love hearing that Horse is dropping by when he sits next to me in the small rocker and asks what's wrong with her. I try to bluff him but he's having none of it and says come on, he's got eyes. I tell him, then say that after the surgery there might be chemo, then the waiting. When he asks the size of the tumor I tell him it's small, it's nothing to worry about.

"Well, that's good," he answers, playing along. I ask him not to mention to Helen that he knows and he says he wouldn't do that for anything. When I say this is your day he tells me he knows that and adds as he goes inside that this is one hell of a real world. Then the early-morning street is like a half-finished painting, the pinks and light greens wash together, and there comes a hush that makes the light a part of the brain. The only movement is from two gulls riding a high early current over the motels on Beach Avenue.

When Helen comes out she's in navy-blue Bermuda shorts and a white golf shirt and she's already done her make up. She looks lovely as she sets her coffee cup on the railing and then turns to me and says for this whole day we aren't going to talk about it. In answer, I tell her Horse is coming and she says sternly, "Fine, so long as he doesn't stay for lunch."

"Got that," I say.

Then I ask if she wants to bike down to Convention Hall in a while and watch the start of the race. She nods and says afterwards she's going to get her hair done and go to the Acme for the shrimp, baked ham and macaroni salad.

It's right then that Horse drives up in what must be a 20-year-old Cadillac convertible and parks in front of the house. As he comes up the steps carrying a small duffle bag in one hand and a chocolate Tasty Cake in the other, he looks no different—auburn hair, sharp blue eyes, face flushed—from three months ago when he stopped by in Metuchen Easter Sunday. He finishes the Tasty Cake at the top of the steps, drops the bag, and says, chewing, "Jack Henderson and the missus." As he shakes my hand he looks at Helen. Right away he reads she's not overjoyed to see him and he says quickly he's not looking to mooch a meal or a night's stay like last time, only to change for the race and with her kind permission to shower afterwards. He bows, but Helen doesn't fool around with him and says straight out that Gary's getting married this afternoon and there'll be 12 people here in three hours. "I'll be long gone," Horse says, then turns to me like she's disappeared and says how the hell are you. I ask if he's still putting on Tupperware parties in south Jersey, and he answers he's in fire extinguishers now and asks if I'd like to see his line, it's in the trunk, everything from industrials to the new mini Quick-Out for cars and boats. I glance down to the Cadillac and see the rear is so low it could be holding bricks. "You've been radon mitigated?" he asks, and I laugh and say, "Horse, I'm not buying." Then he looks at Helen, who's ignoring him, eyes in the street, and it's like he knows something's wrong. As his eyes come back at me it seems he's reached some intuitive conclusion, and he's lost a lot of his cheeriness. After another long sideways look at Helen he says he's been running since February, then adds this'll be his first 10K, picked for its flatness. He raises the duffel bag slightly and says he'll just go and change, and as soon as he's inside Helen turns and gives me a look that says if he stays for lunch my marriage is over.

After about ten minutes Horse calls out from deep inside the house to ask if he can have a hunk of that gorgeous chocolate cake. Helen's out of her chair and into the house so fast that the screen door nearly comes off its hinges. Going down the hall I hear her shout, "Don't you touch that," followed by Horse saying, "Okay, okay." I imagine he's backing away from the dining room table, hands raised, as if Helen's holding a gun on him. In a few moments he comes out in jogging shorts and a tank top, glances back through the screen door, and then, his voice lowered, says, "None of my business, but what's with her?"

For some reason I can not help myself and in one sentence tell him. "Oh," he concludes, "she's scared." I say she sure is, but nobody's about to know it. When he says, "Keep that stuff in and it makes it worse," I can only nod. "What she needs," he goes on, "is for someone to hit her over the head." Then he's down the stairs in a flash and I watch him jog down New York Avenue in the direction of Convention Hall. After a few moments I go inside and see that Horse has used the small living room to the right with the bathroom off it, his clothes spread out on the couch and floor, dropped where they came off.

On the boardwalk in front of Convention Hall, which is above the street by eight feet or so, Helen is utterly removed from the activity of the hundreds of runners warming up. "Know what he did?" she says after a quiet time. It takes a moment to realize she's referring to Horse and I say no. "He put his hands on my shoulders and asked me what was wrong, asked if he could do anything."

"What'd you tell him?" I say.

"Nothing, that I'm *fine*." She drops her head and shakes it a little, then raises it. Her eyes are watery again but she's stiff and in control. She smiles and says the big grunt kissed her in the middle of the forehead and said, "'Sure there is.' Then he said he loved me," she adds. After a moment she says she's going to the other side of the boardwalk between Morrow's and Convention Hall to look at the ocean. I ask if she wants me to come and she shakes her head and walks off alone. I watch her lean on the railing with her forearms, head up, her hair tossed by the updraft, and I know I can't do anything for her.

As the starter down below calls through his megaphone

that it's two minutes to race time I realize Gary was right when he predicted the high humidity would make the race difficult. Just before the start the light shore wind stops as if by a switch, and I know that inland, which is most of the race, the sun will make the top of the head burn. There are six to seven hundred runners and it's difficult to pick out Gary, Sally and Louis up near the front. But Horse is easy to spot because he's lined up dead last, right in front of the trail convertible and the rescue truck behind it. He and a thin muscular man wearing a white baseball cap, who must be in his 70's, are talking, both with hands on hips. My guess is that Horse is assessing his fire-extinguisher needs. At the start as Horse goes by I wave and at first he doesn't see me, then does. "Go get 'em," I call down and, jogging slowly, he looks at me and gives the thumbs-up sign with both hands, then calls back, "Piece of cake." He holds my eyes with his, as if asking a question, until he's well past where I am. I turn as Helen comes back, her eyes huge and watery, and when I ask if she's all right she nods and says of course, but she's behind schedule right now and she'd better get going. I answer I'll go with her because I've decided to go up to the bandstand in the park for the finish. "It's still exciting, isn't it?" she says. It is, I answer, my eyes on the mass of people strung out ten and twelve across several hundred yards away.

Later, at the park, spectators are already two and three deep in the narrow parking lot at the finish, a water truck and Bud van parked on the grass. Above the finish line is a huge digital clock, its numbers in bright red and white, the tenths spinning in a blur. Right now it's pulsing through minute 25 and under it one of the officials with a walkie-talkie and hand-held loudspeaker announces that the lead runner is just passing the Golden Eagle on Beach Avenue, only two blocks up from our house, and that there could be a new record. I imagine the leader so free that he leaps into the air and starts up a long invisible ramp, a man who knows time has no meaning and who's decided the clock can spin itself to death, he's going to race the clouds across the sky. But about eight minutes later when he rounds the corner and speeds toward the finish his eyes are riveted on the clock, the pain on his face as though there's broken glass in his Nikes. Two officials confirm a hand-held time two seconds faster than last year—a new record, indeed. More interesting is how much he's won by—a good 200 yards I'd guess, and as he stands just beyond the finish line, hands on hips now, breathing in great gulps, he looks back, arrogant and invincible, at those approaching.

In the middle of the pack Gary, Sally and Louis all finish together looking as though throughout the race they haven't done much more than have a pleasant, forty-five-minute conversation. I bring them water and they're hardly breathing, although the sweat makes their skin slick and shiny. Gary says it was hotter back near the small vegetable farms than it's ever been, probably over a hundred in the sun, and they went by a bunch of runners who'd gone out too fast and gotten into trouble. Sally says they heard the siren on the rescue truck three or four times. I look around for Horse, but don't see him. I remember then that five or six years ago a doctor from right here in town died during the race. Louis, who now seems to feel more of the effects of the race, sits down on the curb, legs straight out, and says it was damn brutal out there. After another few moments they decide to go straight to the ocean to cool down and I say I'll see them back at the house. As they go I turn to see the trail convertible just coming round the corner, the older man who was with Horse methodically plodding along to the applause of the crowd. He's taken off his shirt, which is wadded in his right hand, and with the left he raises his cap to everyone. He looks the same as when he began.

It's not until I get back to the house that I realize I didn't see Horse because he didn't finish. His clothes are gone and the car, too, and it's my guess that he bailed out of the race along Beach Avenue and walked back to the house. When Helen gets in, both rear baskets on the bike so full that coming up the gravel driveway she wobbles and nearly falls, she's delighted Horse is gone. As we both unload the bike she makes one crack about Horse being all she needed today and then drops it.

I'm not two seconds back out on the porch sitting in the rocker when I hear Helen scream. It's not as if someone's burned a hand or badly cut a thumb, but, rather, a moment of true despair. I tear inside and down the hall to the kitchen but Helen's not there. I turn instantly at the sob I hear from the dining room and see her staring at the space where a six-inch wedge has been cut from the chocolate cake. "*No, no,*" she says and turns to me, both hands white fists in front of her chest. As she collapses into me sobbing, "Oh, God, I'm so afraid, I'm so afraid," in my mind I see Horse in his convertible flying up the Garden State knowing finally that he doesn't owe me a thing.

WAITING FOR LOUIS

On this very mild late December afternoon Helen and I are walking the beach, the clouds out over the water like long, rolled pillows, the light ancient. Helen, walking a little behind me in a navy blue windbreaker, arms folded, head down, has hardly said a word since the call two hours ago from Louis in which he told her that he and his wife of three years were separating—actually already had a week ago—and he was on his way here from the Massachusetts prep school where he's taught English for the last four years.

Helen has taken the news as if she's just been told of the sudden death of a loved one, her voice with a bitterness I've seldom heard in all the years we've been married. She goes on as if *I've* said something: "God, Jack, you just don't throw away a marriage." Her words are muffled a little by a sudden rise of wind off the water, and as I turn back toward her it's as if deep inside her an important nerve has been burned away. I stop and within a step and a half she's next to me and I put an arm across her shoulders. Her arms are still folded so tightly that I can feel how the long thin muscles of her shoulders are turning to ropes. "Just please," she says, eyes so tense and dark it's as though they're trying to make holes in the sand. She responds not at all to the small pressure of my arm, nor to the wind through her hair. She stares out at the horizon, the colors of the afternoon now gray muscled on gray.

We walk around the ends of the next two jetties, the only remarks between us things like how wonderful Louis and Penny seemed back in late August when they were here with Gary's family and us for a long weekend—"like they'd just been married," Helen says—then adds, "for God's sake," and my saying what a hell of a shock it is, and that, frankly, I don't understand it. "People have hard times," Helen says, "but so what?" As if she wants to say more but no right words will come, she settles for, "I mean, so what?" Helen suddenly stops and says she knows what the problem is, and before I can say anything she explains it's the isolation of where they live, that Penny's from Manhattan and had always lived and worked there, that back in August she told her that that damn school was in Timbuktu. I answer that I don't think that's it, not at all, that they get away to Boston or back to New York every other weekend. "Not in the winter," Helen says, "not in the winter."

I shake my head, even raise a finger chest high, then say, "My guess's that the issue's children." I follow this with a couple of conclusive nods, feel my mouth set into a firm line. Helen's clearly surprised. I remind her that over Labor Day, when they'd gone back, we talked about how distant—actually, I used the word, *aloof*—Penny was around Gary's boys. Helen nods and says that possibly I'm right, that so far as she can remember Penny hardly ever went near them. Then Helen has a second thought and says that, after all, Gary's sons are—"well," she says after a short pause—"unruly. Especially when they're here." I smile and say *demons* is more like it, then recall how they each dumped a bucket of ocean water on Penny while she was napping under our umbrella. "Called them *les gamins*," I say, my French pretty poor. Helen's actually smiling and looks as though she's relaxing a little. Behind her there's a group of perhaps 50 gulls facing west as though they're in some kind of squadron, all standing perfectly still on one leg. "And how on Sunday they tried to untie her top," she says, now with a smile. She turns around and looks at the gulls as though all along she's known they were there, settling in.

Then a wave of sadness comes over Helen and, after a moment, me, too. It's as if we both feel the weather suddenly turning, but it's not. Helen gives me a short glance, then looks away at the water and the last of the light lying right on top of it. "Now you take Gary and Sally," she says, but then, as if someone's whispering to her to be quiet, she stops, drops her head, and kicks away a small mound of sand.

We walk the two blocks back to the house, and as we turn onto New York Avenue I see that ours is the only house on the block with a light on—the single bulb on the ceiling of the porch right over the front door. It is like a stark beacon in the night that, the longer you look at it, the more it tells you it has no message. Beside me, head down, Helen is crying a little, her sounds private and directed inward, the kind of crying that over the years, when it's happened, I've learned I can do nothing about.

Inside, without a word, Helen goes upstairs to make up Louis's bedroom, and I know that she will do it with great care, that the bed will have her good linen, and that on the old dresser she will lay out matching towels and a washcloth in a small, delicate pile. She will raise the shades to exactly half way on both windows, set the closet door slightly ajar, and put on the bedside lamp, its shade covered with 20 or 30 small sailboats. It's been right there on the night table just like that since he and Gary were kids.

Standing in the huge empty hall, one foot on the heating grate in the middle of the floor, I listen to her movements above me and a little to the left. It could be any year, it could be any time we've ever been here. I call up to ask again what time he said he'd be here, and Helen surprises me when, at the top of the stairs, just on the way down, she says, as if she's been thinking about it for some minutes, "And the way she says snow, says, '*snew*,' for God's sake." This has never registered with me until now, and, after a second or two, I say, "Yes, she does. Sure does." Although I know it's not really possible except when the wind's absolutely just right in the summer I'm sure I hear the low dull sound of waves breaking. Then I wonder just what it is I'm listening for.

Helen turns at the bottom of the stairs and as if I'm really not there at all starts back to the kitchen. Halfway down the hall she says it's chicken tonight, maybe in an hour or so. "I'll save some for Louis," she says. Suddenly, from nowhere, I feel as though I'm outside in the middle of the night, the darkness like a sullen arm from deep space reaching out for everything. From the kitchen Helen calls out that later, after we eat, she's got to go down to the Acme and get tomato juice and eggs and bacon for the morning— and raisin bread for toast—all Louis's favorites. I answer that it'll be good to see him and she calls back, "It will. Yes."

What, I wonder, are all these spaces for, these patches of nothingness among us, unbridgeable and austere.

And then I am judging Louis, and Penny, too, people who, I think, are not willing to—and the word comes to me from some of the times Helen and I have had—*endure.* Those times swirl back, periods of weeks, sometimes even months, when a glacier formed between us, the great magic of it all hidden in the mystery of its one day simply being gone. Have Louis and Penny, I wonder, just given up after only a few years, a time in the beginning when Helen and I hardly even knew each other. It comes to me that Helen and I have been married thirty-four years, and all that matters in all of it is this very second.

Right next to me on the hall table the phone rings, its sound amplified greatly, or so it seems, by the high ceiling and hardwood floor. I pick up the receiver expecting it to be Louis with a specific time he'll be here, but it's Penny, her voice unsteady. She says my name, and then asks if we've heard. I say yes, we have, and then ask how she is, if she's all right. Out of the corner of my eye I see Helen standing in the kitchen doorway, holding a dishtowel with both hands, absolutely still. Penny asks if Louis is there, and I tell her no, but he's on his way, in my voice a helplessness that all I can do is supply a lousy fact or two for her. I turn to look at Helen, her face tense, eyes straight on me as though she's lost the power to blink. I tell Penny that we expect him sometime this evening, and then quickly ask if she wants him to call. "I'm at my mother's," she says, then adds, "Thanks," and, so formally, says, "Goodbye, Jack."

It takes Helen a moment to realize that I'm holding a dead phone, and then she says, "What'd she say?" expectation in her voice. She sounds as if I'm keeping important information from her, and she prods me with,

"Well?" As I set the phone down I say, without looking at her, that she wants to talk to Louis, that she's in New York. "And?" Helen asks.

"Just that," I answer.

Helen snaps the dishtowel out of one hand and it dangles by her side for a second or two before she turns and steps back into the kitchen.

Through the living room window to my right, its glass so old that everything seen through it is slightly rippled and, in some places, truly distorted, I catch a glimpse of the street light now behind a huge sheet of fog. I know that up on Beach Avenue the ocean's gone, the great line of yellow lights all the way down to the arcades strung out like old, useless stars, the street and boardwalk shiny and absolutely empty. I remember our honeymoon here, the second or third night it was—and late, too—when there was this kind of fog, only warmer, and Helen and I, so full of joy we could not sleep, walked down to the beach without saying a word, as though we owned the whole damn thing.

As I walk over to the window, the light dancing on the old glass, Helen calls out to ask if I want peas or broccoli. I answer whatever she wants, the room-to-room talk feeling as if it's over a much greater distance. "Actually," I call back, "the peas." I look up the street toward Pittsburgh as far as I can see, which is only to the second street light in the next block. I want to see Louis's old Jetta coming along New York Avenue, its lights bobbing as it goes over the years-old frost heaves in the asphalt.

"Louis doesn't like peas," Helen says from down the hall. It comes back to me that when he was a small child I, stubborn as hell, tried to make him eat them at dinner one night. It was not about peas, Helen said to me later, but about control. Louis won, hands down. "Then the broccoli,"

I say just loud enough to get to her. "By all means."

When the phone rings again Helen hurries down the hall to it. I know even before she says hello that it's Louis. She'll tell me after she hangs up in a few minutes that he's in a Roy Rogers off the Garden State, about two hours away, that he called Penny's mother's place but only got the machine, that when she told him Penny called here all he said was, "Oh?"

"That's it," she says, looking at me as if I have a simple, final answer to everything but have decided not to tell her what it is.

"Then we can have the peas?" I ask, my voice rising at the end, trying to be light.

When there's no response from her except a tiny glance in my direction I ask if he said anything else, said maybe how he was doing. Helen looks lost, her eyes on the floor. Then she shakes her head and, without looking at me, goes back down the hall to the kitchen. "Maybe they'll work it out," I say. "They're young, they might be able to do that."

"For God's sakes," she says, "everybody *thinks* about it." Her voice has the same neutral quality it did when she asked about the peas, then I step over to the living room doorway and lean against one of the old tall pocket doors. With my voice only very slightly raised, I say, tentatively, "For sure." I look down the hall to see that she's standing just inside the kitchen, head down, the dishtowel wound severely around her hands.

"Why do people stay together at all?" she suddenly asks, the question, by its tone, directed away from me, toward some general, unseen audience. When I say a lot don't she nods, still not looking at me, and then says, "But those who do, why?" I tell her I don't think anyone knows, I say I think it's all supposed to be a mystery. "Acts of will," she says, then adds that she means in the good sense, not like the Cranemores who fight at least once a day and are sarcastic to each other in front of others. She waves a hand to dismiss them, then adds, "All the regular people who love each other."

"Well, there you have it," I say. "Love it is." As though I've said nothing, she turns slowly, perhaps, I think, hearing something I can't, and disappears back into the kitchen.

After a minute, when the skillet has finally hit the burner and she's starting to slide it around to melt the butter, she says, "Nobody knows a damn thing about love."

I manage a *huh?* from where I am, and, as if she's given it all a lot of thought, she says, "Look at all the kinds there are. Nobody knows what it is." She says this in a way that's dismissive, as if there's nothing more to discuss on the subject.

While I take a couple of steps to the front door to look out again at the fog, she goes on to say that, after all, you don't love your dog the way you love your mother, you don't love a spouse like you love a kid.

Then she's quiet, and I have no trouble imagining that she's standing right in front of the stove staring at the searing chicken breasts wondering what fell apart in Louis's and Penny's lives. I think of them getting married here, like Gary and Sally did, the intensely personal vows each wrote, how they could not take their eyes off each other that day. And how they looked—as if they'd known each other all their lives, had already grown close in mannerisms and looks, were somehow quickly settling into each other.

"I'm going to be very sad about all of this," Helen calls out. I see a car coming slowly along New York Avenue from Pittsburgh, and although I know it can't be Louis, I imagine that it is, that he guides the car to a stop in front of the house, gets out and hurries up the steps to where we're both waiting for him. I may not, in this moment, know what love is, but that'll do for now.

SEEING VERNA

About an hour ago I just left the house and walked the two blocks down to the beach. I did this for two reasons: one is that Alzheimer's is finally in full possession of Mary, who's probably still sitting on the porch and who barely recognizes her daughters—tomorrow we'll put her in the Seaview Manor over in Wildwood Crest—and the other is my know-everything brother-in-law, Dennis, who, along with Maureen, drove down yesterday from Red Bank. Maureen's a fine person, now at 52 about five ten and 160, her red hair and freckles complementing her quick laugh and sharp blue eyes.

I'm coming the long way around back to the house: Beach Avenue to Madison, then doubling back, wasting time on purpose. Two blocks up Madison the late afternoon sun dims behind a distant bank of huge rising clouds that looks like the Rockies in winter. It's June and all along our block come the early summer sounds of lawn mowers, hammers, power saws and drills. It seems ironic that it was three years ago today, when we got back from my mother, Verna's, funeral in Altoona, that we realized something wasn't right with Mary, whom we hadn't seen since Christmas. There was a dent in the right front fender of her impeccably kept Ford Escort, which she hadn't fixed because she kept forgetting it, and at dinner here that night she mixed up the names of our and Maureen's children. But already she'd learned to cover herself, saying she was forgetful these days and it wasn't fair being 84 and all alone.

Until about two weeks ago Mary was doing all right in her own house in Wildwood, having declined, indeed, disdained, invitations to live with us or Maureen and Dennis, with the help of a 12-hour aide and a long-time neighbor who came in to make dinner and sleep over. But when the inevitable happened—a week ago tomorrow the police found Mary at six in the morning in bathrobe and slippers standing at the window of a McDonald's drive-thru waiting for it to open—Helen and Maureen came down to stay with her, talk to her doctor, and make the arrangements for the Seaview.

Maureen and Helen treat Mary as if nothing's wrong, which I didn't understand until I realized it was their way of still loving her. But when I've tried to do the same it's been more difficult because she looks at me, smiles pleasantly, and says, "Hello, young man." And when I've been sitting with her on the porch—someone has to be with her all the time—she's asked what I do for a living. When I tell her, and add that Helen's still a librarian, she always says she thinks that's so nice.

As I come up the steps she's in a white blouse, red skirt and new sneakers sitting with Dennis. One knee-hi has bunched around an ankle. He says hi, Jack, and asks if I've had a good walk. Mary looks over at me and smiles as if I'm delivering something. I say hello and then go inside and into the small living room where Helen's right next to Maureen on the couch, both crying softly, knees touching. Maureen looks up at me and says, very slowly, "She is *so* pathetic." Helen changes the Kleenex ball from one hand to the other and with the free one takes Maureen's hand and says she feels like she's at my mother's funeral.

Dennis comes in from the porch and asks what the problem is and when Maureen says, "*Guess*," Dennis raises his hands like a calming preacher, and tells her, as he did last night, that what we're doing with Mary is for the best. Maureen answers that Mary thinks she's here for a two-day visit with all of us and tomorrow morning she and Helen are going to betray her like two Judases. "Hokum," Dennis answers.

"Leave it," Helen says.

Not Dennis. He begins a short history of Mary's illness in the way a small child accomplished with blocks starts a project, but it doesn't take Maureen long before she shuts him off with, "Please?" then hangs her head and lets another wave of sorrow sweep through her. But when Dennis says he agrees with how sad the situation is but that these things happen all the time, Helen realizes that Mary's alone and she gets up and goes into the hall and out the front door. I turn and give Dennis a look I hope he can read the message in, then follow Helen. Even before I push open the screen door I know Mary's gone. Helen's on the top step looking up and down the street, her body more tense than I've ever seen it. "You see her?" I ask as I come up behind her. She shakes her head frantically, then softly says oh, my God. I turn and call loudly for Maureen and Dennis, and just as they come through the door I tell them Mary's disappeared. "Well," Dennis says, going down the steps, "she couldn't have gone very far." He turns and looks up at Maureen, then says leaving Mary alone was thoughtless and what was he thinking. Maureen doesn't hear the second part because she's already halfway through the door to call the police, and Helen, now down in the middle of the street, hands on hips as she looks both ways, doesn't hear him, either.

I go back into the house and through the kitchen, then out to the small back porch to make certain Mary hasn't just gone around the house or wandered into Colonel Wilberforce's yard next door. Nothing. Back inside and coming through the hall, Maureen's just finishing her call and tells me someone's on the way. "He's a jerk like that sometimes," she says and as we go out front again I ignore the remark and say maybe Mary's back. Proof that she isn't is in Dennis's just getting into the Saab and waving to Maureen to come quickly. Helen's already in the Taurus doing the same to me. Their plan is to go in opposite directions circling the long blocks very slowly. Maureen gets in but I tell Helen someone has to stay here for the police, and then she quickly shifts into *Drive*, cramps the wheel for a *u*, and speeds off. I look up toward Madison, then the other way to Pittsburgh, let my eyes stay in each direction for a moment hoping I might see Mary. The street is strangely empty for this time of day.

It's as I turn to go back up the steps to the porch that I'm dumbfounded to see Mary just opening the screen door. She sees me, smiles, and says, "Hello, young man," then walks back to where she's been sitting all afternoon. As I come up the steps I ask her where she's been and she looks at me as though I've asked the square root of 27. Well, I tell her anyway, you've given us quite a scare. Same look. I know then from the dark water spots on her skirt and her wet hands that while we were all in the living room Mary had simply come in quietly and gone to the bathroom. As I sit next to her she gives me the kind of warm open smile I remember from years ago when she'd come over from Wildwood to baby-sit our sons while we went to a movie. "Now," she says, legs crossed, hands joined in her lap, "I know I know you." When I tell her I'm Helen's husband she registers the fact with a nod, and when I say my name she answers, "Oh, yes," and looks out to the street. After a moment she says, "Verna?" and I say yes, she was my mother. She smiles and says, "How is she?" I stop myself from saying she's dead and nod and smile a little and say she's all right. Mary says she's a nice person and that she likes her a lot and then asks if she's coming soon. I answer no, she won't be able to this summer. "We had such nice times," she says.

Just then the police car comes to a stop at the curb and immediately I go down to explain. The officer looks up at Mary for a long moment and when I turn I see her smiling at us. He's not out of his twenties, the hair at the sides of his head as short as a Marine's. He says his grandmother's like that, too, then shakes my hand, gets back in the car, and leaves. As I go up the steps Mary's smile continues, and I expect her to ask what the police wanted. Instead, she says, "Hello, young man." I say hi as though I've been at work all day and sit down again. We have the same conversation, only this time I tell her Verna died and she turns to me and says, "Oh." Then almost immediately she settles back in her chair and once more gazes into the street. After a moment, she asks what time dinner will be, and I tell her about seven we're going to the Lobster House for take-out flounder and fries and eat at the wooden tables set out on the wharf. She tells me she and Mel used to drive over from Wildwood just for the flounder. There's a moment's pause and she leans toward me and says he died. When I answer I know she looks at me carefully, then asks if I knew him. I tell her I'm her son-in-law and she seems surprised, but then says of course I am and puts a hand on my arm.

Helen is first back, but she doesn't see Mary and me until she comes around the front of the car. It's clear she's been crying, and she starts again as she comes up the steps and over to Mary saying where'd you go, then looking at me and saying where'd you find her. Mary asks what's the matter and Helen says she's sorry she left her alone, she won't do it again. I tell Helen what happened just as Maureen and Dennis drive up and park. Right away they see Mary's okay and Dennis hollers up to ask, "How's the little lady?"

It's just as the low sun starts to make dull, wavy lightning on the oily water in front of the wharf that Maureen decides it's time Mary knows what's going to happen tomorrow. She asks a series of gentle questions about forgetfulness and who makes her meals, etc., which requires Mary to convict herself, but it's meaningless because by the time Maureen's finished, and satisfied with herself, Mary's forgotten what they started to talk about. Then Dennis says flatly to Mary that in his opinion she can't take care of herself anymore, to which Mary answers she's certainly getting along all right. Helen takes Mary's hand and asks if she remembers getting lost last week. Mary stares at her and says no such thing happened. Dennis says it certainly did and looks away to follow the legs of the college girl who's just brought his second gin and tonic. Then when Helen says she and Maureen, and Dennis and I, too, want her to be safe and cared for in the Seaview, it's as if an invisible wall in front of Mary disappears. She says, "In that place?" on her face a moment of panic. We neither do nor say anything, and the silence hits her hard. "*No*," she says.

"You must be safe," Helen tells her so lovingly it's as though she's able to compress years of feeling. Somehow, Mary senses Helen's concern and looks at her for a long moment. Then she says, "Has it come to this?" Helen takes one hand, Maureen the other, each in her lap, and Mary sits back with a sweet, sad calm on her face. "Ice cream?" Maureen says. It's at that moment, the twilight just about to go, that I swear I see my mother come out the front door of the Lobster House with a tall man, both in love and leaning on each other. They hold hands all the way to the parking lot.

Maureen and Helen prepare Mary for bed as if she were a toddler. Dennis and I on the porch just below the window hear the hair dryer and their soft laughter. We hear more the tone of their voices than the content, its low steady sound comforting under Dennis's chatter about the difference between the Seaview's bills and Medicare. There's a silence then as if the dark around us is about to speak, not a sound from upstairs, not a distant car nor a touch of wind, the kind of pause before cells divide. It feels like the purest moment one might know, time a globe I can hold in my hands.

In the morning the five of us go in our car, Mary between Helen and Maureen in the back, Dennis next to me. Mary has no idea where we're going, but she believes this to be a special event. In the mirror I can see her fiddling with her chin first with one hand, then the other.

The Seaview is not much to look at on the outside and has a view of the ocean only from the third floor rear. Inside, though, there is a pleasant, orderly calm, not at all like the hospital setting I'd imagined, the nurses and attendants in bright, flower-colored smocks with small white name tags, soft living-room lighting everywhere but the *Intake* office we go to first. Helen, a folder with Mary's medical records under her arm, goes in while the three of us sit with Mary in the small area just outside. The door stays open and I have a view of Helen and the nursing director, a tall gray-haired man with wire-rim glasses, sitting across from each other at a desk. After a few moments he turns and faces the computer and begins to put the information into it that Helen gives him, some of which she has to refer to the folder for. In the next few moments there is the same quiet I felt last night. Helen gets up and comes to the door to ask if I remember the year Mel died, and I'm astonished I can't instantly recall it but, rather, have to remember that our older son, Gary, had just been born. I tell her that and as she nods Mary says the month, day and year, then says Helen and I ought to remember because we were at the house with the baby visiting. Behind Helen the gray-haired man nods, smiles, and taps away.

Then we get a tour of the home, and we see that everything one could need is supplied. Dennis rightly observes that it's comfortable. What is not for me are the people in the place, "our guests," the director calls them, who are everywhere we go, their infirmities plain to see: double hearing aids, the fixed pupils of macular degeneration, the walkers and canes, the heavy stares of those who simply don't know where they are, the men and women with diaper bulges under their polyester trousers and slacks.

Our parting with Mary is quick and unexpected. The director leaves us in Mary's room, second floor front, having shown us the bath and toilet and indicated that Mary's bed is closer to the window. The two suitcases we'd left in the small waiting room are already beside her bed and so swiftly do the two aides come in as he leaves that I know the procedure is planned. The windows look out on the parking lot, a well-kept hedge bordering it, in the near distance several blocks of small shore homes, mostly white. When Dennis says it's time we were on our way Mary sits heavily on the bed and puts her face in her hands. Maureen stares at Dennis who spreads his arms slightly and says, "Well, when?" I take Dennis by the elbow and we go into the hall where he asks what the heck did he say wrong. When I tell him our wives want to say goodbye to their mother he says what am I talking about, they can come back this afternoon if they want. "I know," I answer.

We drive back to Cape May with Dennis next to me, Helen and Maureen in the back, and no one says anything. It's midmorning, the tide so high that through the inlet the water is right next to the road. The toll collector on the narrow, two-lane bridge says it's going to be a hot one, although it doesn't feel like it yet. Driving down Pittsburgh Maureen tells Helen she's coming back next weekend to see Mary and start through her house. They make it a date, and then Dennis asks what about John Browning's barbecue. Maureen says he can go if he likes. "We didn't have any choice, did we?" Helen asks Maureen. In the mirror I see her put two nervous fingers on her chin, then take them away. Dennis answers of course not, then adds it was the right and proper thing to do. "Humane," he says. Maureen tells him to be quiet, adding in something close to a whisper, "For God's sake." Dennis then turns and tells me his parents are 88 and 86 and still living in Boca. "Fit as fiddles," he says, then adds for a reason I can't comprehend that they've already picked out and paid for their urns. "She's going to die there," Helen says, the words absolutely even, almost cold. I expect either Maureen or Dennis to answer, but when I glance into the mirror I see in her eyes that the statement's for me. I can not bring myself to use words but, instead, nod once slowly.

I park right behind the Saab and Maureen and Dennis get out and head up the steps quickly, their plans to leave for home already an hour behind. As Helen gets out she puts a hand on my shoulder and asks if I'm all right. I nod and say sure and then she leaves, the sound of her door closing precise and perfect. In the sun the heat builds in the car right away, the air like blood. A VW goes by on the other side of the street and makes no sound. I'm sure I get another glimpse of Verna, the short white hair, hands high on the wheel, nose forward. Before I catch myself I actually wonder where she's going. With the heat the silence comes again, this time in an easy, smooth way, and I am more accepting of it than last night or even a little while ago. It sounds like eternity.

With Maureen and Dennis gone Helen and I walk down to Philadelphia Beach. She asks just as we cross Beach Avenue if she and Maureen did the right thing, and I tell her yes, what else was there to do? She says Mary couldn't come to live with us because we couldn't take care of her, then reminds me the doctor told her Mary'd need real care within a few months with things like her toilet, bath and feeding. I know, I tell her. As we go down the ramp there's suddenly a stiff south wind off the cool water, whitecaps far out, a schooner, its sails full of sun, a few hundred yards off the jetty. As we start across the sand to the edge of the water she takes my hand. "She'll be all right," I tell her, my voice utterly flat. It's then we see the eight or ten black fire rings from the after-prom party last night, bits of charred hot dogs and marshmallows half buried in the black sand. The circles seem like the centers of primitive homes, and I'm surprised the tide has not cleaned everything away.

I tell Helen about the two times since yesterday I've imagined seeing Verna and she turns and looks up at me and says she'd forgotten this week was the anniversary of her death. Then she asks if I know how long it's been since we've made love and I tell her I do. Her hand curls as it goes all the way up my arm and she leans her head into my shoulder. "Remember," she says, "how that used to solve everything?"

The stories in this collection were originally published, in slightly different form, in the following journals and literary reviews:

"Shore Light," *The Southeast Review*, Vol. 14, No. 1

"Grief and Fire," *The Cimarron Review*, No. 106

"Stop Signs," *Oasis*, Vol. X, No. IV

"Upwelling," *Interim*, Vol. 13, No. 2

"A Message From Mel," *The Green Hills Literary Lantern*, Issue No. Six

"Three's A Crowd," *The New Orleans Review*, 29.2

"The Right To Sing," *BookPress*, Vol. 9, No. 2

"Human D.," *The Ledge Fiction and Poetry Review*, No. 20

"Middle Age," *Other Voices*, Vol. 11, No. 28

"Debts," *Button*, No. 12

"Waiting For Louis," *The Nebraska Review*, Vol. 31, No. 2

"Seeing Verna," *Meridian*, Issue 10

ABOUT THE AUTHOR

Robert C.S. Downs has published six novels and has had one screenplay produced by CBS Television. Three of his novels have been produced by NBC, CBS and the BBC. He has taught in the MFA programs at The University of Arizona and Penn State University. A former Guggenheim Fellow in fiction writing, he was also an NAACP Image Award nominee. *The Cape May Stories* is his first collection of short fiction. He lives in State College, Pennsylvania.

If you enjoyed
The Cape May Stories
you may enjoy

Big Five-O Cafe (James Wolfe)
Junk Lottery (Mickey Getty)
Manual for Normal (Rebecca McEldowney)
Sitka Incident: Exxon Valdez Retold (Walt Larson)
Soldier in a Shallow Grave (Gerald Cline)
Soul of Flesh (Rebecca McEldowney)

Please visit
www.windstormcreative.com/fiction/
for a complete selection